ON THE SQUARE

University Square, Book One

Brenda Murphy

A NineStar Press Publication

www.ninestarpress.com

On the Square

Printed in the USA

Print ISBN: 978-1-64890-070-9

First Edition, August, 2020

Also available in eBook, ISBN: 978-1-64890-069-3

WARNING:
This book contains sexually explicit material which is only suitable for mature readers, racism, homophobia, homophobic violence.

Dropped from her television show after a very public split with her cheating ex, celebrity chef Mai Li wants nothing more than to reopen her parents' shuttered restaurant and make a fresh start in her former hometown. So what if twenty years of neglect has left the building in need of a major renovation?

Seduced by Mai's charm and determination, hard-edged contractor Dale Miller agrees to take on her renovation project.

After a spring storm causes significant damage to the building and renovation costs exceed Mai's budget, Dale offers her a deal, but is it a price Mai is willing to pay?

To C, Always.

Chapter One

Dale filled her coffee thermos. The scent of the dark brew had her wanting to linger over another cup. She tightened the lid. "You riding the bus today?"

"Nah, Chip's coming to pick me up. We have a cross-country team meeting." Noah slid the omelet he was cooking onto the plate. "You sure you don't have time? You can have this one, Mom. I'll cook another for me." His round face and solemn dark-brown eyes were fixed on her face. He lifted the plate and waved it in her direction.

Delicately browned, perfectly cooked. The aroma of melted cheddar cheese and butter filled the small kitchen. The omelet tempted Dale even more than the coffee had. She sighed and cursed herself for agreeing to an early morning appointment for an estimate. Dale grimaced. Cowed by the insistence of the woman who called for the estimate, her oldest, Seth, had made the appointment outside of business hours. *Afraid to turn down work. Knows we need the money. If it works out.*

Dale tucked two peanut butter and strawberry jelly sandwiches into her cooler, wrapped an apple in a napkin, and placed three battered and scruffy water bottles around the sides, spacing them evenly. She shut the lid and bungeed the ancient metal relic of a cooler shut. *Please let it work out.*

"What, Mom?"

The concern in Noah's voice drew Dale from her thoughts. "Nothing. I wish your brother would've talked to me before he scheduled this. I hate to talk to people before I've had my coffee. And who the hell needs to meet at six in the morning for an estimate?" She peered out of the window at the sky, barely pink.

"Someone in a hurry? Like maybe you should be. Or you're gonna be late." Noah smirked as he shoved aside stacks of paper and clutter before he placed his plate on the table. He pulled a chair out, sat down, and flipped his napkin out with a flourish.

"Damn." Dale took two steps over to Noah and mashed a quick kiss to his forehead. "Don't forget to tell Thomas to pick up Grandad's prescription and have a good day at school."

Noah scrubbed his hand over his mouth. "I will."

Dale snatched her thermos and her lunch cooler off the counter as she bolted for the door.

*

The large black pickup truck roared into the parking lot, kicking up a fine spray of dust and small gravel. Mai ended the call she had been ready to make to cancel the estimate appointment and shoved her phone back into her pocket. She frowned as a layer of gray dust settled over her polished black wingtips. Tinted windows prevented her from seeing inside the truck. With a snap of her wrist she straightened her collar, leaned back against her car, and crossed her arms over her chest. She tapped her foot and pursed her lips as she contemplated how much she was going to enjoy telling the yahoo in the truck what she thought of their driving skills. A warm-up for what she was preparing to tell the contractor who didn't think her time was valuable. She didn't do business with people who were not punctual. *This town has not changed a bit. Still on country time.* She snorted thinking about the ridiculous lengths she had to go to get the idiot on the phone to agree to a timely appointment.

The scuff of boots on gravel on the opposite side of the truck made her look up.

"Sorry I'm late." A tall woman in faded jeans and work boots rounded the front of the truck. A thick tan work belt with a multitool pouch clipped to it held her jeans up over her curvy hips. She tucked a metal clipboard under her arm and stuck her hand out to shake.

"Who are you?" Mai didn't take the woman's hand. "I had an appointment with a general contractor for an estimate. Dale Miller?"

"That's me." A flash of irritation flew across Dale's face as she withdrew her hand and stuck it into her rear pocket.

"You're late." Mai studied the unapologetic woman in front of her. Thick honey-blonde hair streaked with gray brushed her shoulders. A head taller than Mai, she had broad shoulders and a trim waist. Her pale-blue undershirt set off her golden-brown eyes. The sleeves of her flannel overshirt were rolled back and displayed well-muscled forearms.

Dale rocked back on her heels and glanced skyward before bringing her gaze back to Mai's face. "I am. And I apologized. This is outside of our normal hours for estimates."

"And I wasn't..."

Dale cut her off. "And you weren't expecting a woman." She swept her hand through her hair. "You know what. I'm not certain I'm the best person for this job." She turned on her heel and walked away from Mai, head high and shoulders rigid.

"Wait."

Dale turned and rested her hand on the hood of the truck. "Why? You've made your mind up. I'm not going to waste my time. Or yours. Good luck with your project."

Mai looked down at her shoes before returning her gaze to Dale's face. "That's not what I was going to say."

"Right." Dale arched an eyebrow. "I've been in this business too long to be scolded for being late. I don't schedule appointments this early because I don't like talking to anyone at this unholy hour."

Mai laughed. "How have you stayed in business?"

Dale walked back over and stepped close to Mai, invading her space. "Because most people in this town recognize business hours are business hours and don't expect special favors."

Mai held her ground. "Special favors? I asked for an early appointment. It's not my fault whoever answered the phone doesn't know your hours."

Dale clenched her fists. "My son knows the hours perfectly well. He was trying to be nice. He said yes to accommodate your schedule. Which, apparently, is way more important than mine. Good day." She spun on her heel and stomped back to the truck.

Mai chewed her lip as she desperately tried to ignore how much she liked the way Dale's ass looked in her jeans and failed. "Hey, wait."

Dale yanked the truck door open and tossed her clipboard inside.

Mai sprinted around the truck and her shoes on skidded on the gravel lot. She caught herself on the truck hood and narrowly avoided bumping into Dale. "Hey, please stay. I'm sorry we got off on the wrong foot. I've had too many folks be rude to me because I wasn't what they expected. Please. I'd like you to at least look at the project."

Dale turned to her and the delicate scent of lemon verbena wafted from her, undermining Mai's determination to keep to the business at hand.

A rueful grin crossed Dale's face. "No. I'm sorry. You'd think I didn't want the work. I'd like to see what you want done." She tilted her head and met Mai's gaze. "Do you mind if we have coffee first?"

Mai held out her hand and Dale shook it. "Bring your thermos." She tilted her head toward the silver flask. "Come on. We don't have to talk until you've had another cup."

*

Mai pulled a set of keys from her pocket as she stood in front of a graffiti-covered gray door set in dull-red bricks. Deep gouges and scratches surrounded the keyhole. She inserted the key, wrestled with the lock a moment, and then shoved her shoulder against the door. It opened with a loud screech. A dark-gray smudge bloomed over her white shirt where her shoulder had contact with the door.

The door opened on to a storeroom. Wire shelves leaned haphazardly against the dirty-white walls. The smell of dust and decay wafted out, laced with the unmistakable scent of some recently dead rodent.

Mai covered her mouth and nose with her hand. "Ugh, that smell."

Dale snagged a broken brick from the parking lot and used it to prop the door open. "This will help." She shrugged at Mai's raised eyebrow. "At least a bit."

They had entered through a kitchen area and now were in the front of the restaurant. The front windows were painted over and the interior was dim. Thick gray dust and bits of plaster were scattered about the floor. Dale wiped a layer of fine debris off the pass-through counter and placed her thermos on it.

"You want some?"

"No, I'm good. I had mine after the gym."

Of course she did. Dale swept her gaze over the Mai's dapper form. Dale guessed Mai was younger by a few years than her forty-two. Tailored black pants and a crisp white shirt with sharp creases draped her frame. A large silver watch wrapped around her slender wrist. Her precisely tapered fade completed the image of a successful young butch about town.

Determined not to dwell on her worn jeans, paint and wood stain-splattered work boots, and basic ten-dollar mom haircut that underscored their differences, Dale focused on unscrewing the top of the thermos. She slammed it onto the counter, tipped the bottle up, and let the smooth taste of the medium roast soothe her. Cheap haircut notwithstanding, Dale didn't mind cutting corners, but she wasn't going to suffer bad coffee.

She studied Mai from under her lashes. A flash of disgust crossed her face and Dale assumed she would have preferred she sip her coffee from the cup, but she wasn't paying for Dale to have manners and Dale certainly didn't have time to care what a customer thought of her behavior. But she had given Dale a second chance after most folks would haven't. *Get it together. For fuck's sake, this job could make our year. Don't blow it.*

Dale turned away from Mai and surveyed the space. Red plastic-covered booths lined one wall of the once popular restaurant. Some of the seats bled stuffing on the floor where the vinyl had ripped. A dozen four-top dark wood tables and chairs were scatted about the area in various states of disrepair. The walls were bare, and wires hung about the faded outlines of framed art long since removed.

"I want to get this back to operating condition." Mai walked about the space as she spoke. "I want to do an open kitchen plan and go back to the original brick." She pointed to the linoleum covered floor. "There are wide board hardwood floors under here. I want to rip all this up and have the floor refinished." A wide smile crossed her face. "I want it to have a retro feel, industrial lights, bright colors." She walked to the front of the restaurant and spread her arms wide. "I want to build a bar here with space for twelve." She walked back to Dale and pulled a folded sheet of paper from her shirt pocket. "Can you make a bar like this? With the different colored wine bottles as part of it? So the light shines through them?"

Dale studied the drawing. "Sure, if my friends and I start drinking now we should have enough to do it."

"What?" Mai peered into Dale's eyes, her forehead furrowed.

"A joke."

"Oh. Right." Mai carefully folded the printout and tucked it back into her pocket.

A silence as thick as the dust settled between them. As Dale sipped her coffee, she scanned the ceiling and studied two large holes which exposed the lath and beams above the kitchen area. "What's upstairs?"

Mai lifted her shoulders and squared them. "Apartments." She raised her gaze to the ceiling. "Two apartments. One with two bedrooms and an efficiency apartment. I want to open the space. Make it one large apartment with two master suites."

"Building this old it was most likely one space to begin with." Dale lifted her hand and pointed to the exposed lath and the beams. "We'll need to make sure the beams are sound before we do anything upstairs." She tilted her head back and took another large swallow of her coffee.

Mai pursed her lips. "Do you think you could salvage the ceiling?" She gestured to the copper ceiling over the front dining room.

"Maybe." Dale took another large swallow of her coffee, its warmth and caffeine setting over her like a balm. Mai walked the length of the dining room and peered out of the front windows with her hands in her pockets. Once Dale had finished her coffee, she capped the thermos and set it aside before she picked up her clipboard. After taking her pen from her shirt pocket she waved at the ceiling. "How do you get to them? Interior or exterior stairs? Might as well start at the top."

"Interior." Mai led the way to a narrow doorway off the back of the kitchen.

Dismally faded multicolor plastic beads hung in the doorway. Some of the dusty strands were missing and broken beads were scattered over the narrow stairs. Mai swept her hand out and down to clear the cobwebs in the doorway before she stepped back and away from the opening. Dale pulled her pocket flashlight out and lit the stairs. "Have you been up here?"

"Not in years." Mai's voice was soft a sharp contrast to the brash woman who had pissed Dale off when she had first arrived. It was the same soft tone Mai had used to convince her she should stay for the estimate.

Dale turned to Mai. "We ate here all the time when I was growing up. I never knew there were apartments. How long've you owned this?" She squinted at Mai. "Are you related to Pop and Mama Li?"

Mai dropped her chin to her chest. "My parents."

Dale chewed her lip. "Sorry, I didn't recognize you. Didn't you go to high school with my baby sister?"

Mai snorted. "Yeah. And don't worry about it. I left home at nineteen. I haven't been back in years. Why would you know me?"

"Weren't you on TV? Had a show? Or something?"

"Yeah. I was." Mai's expression shuttered.

Dale took the hint and bit back the thousand questions her mind served up after Mai's revelation.

Mai glanced at her watch. "We should get moving. I don't want to keep you."

"The steps look okay but stay a bit back and watch your step." Dale moved up the steps, checking each one visually before testing it with her weight. She kicked a mouse carcass to the side. Mai's grunt of disgust echoed in the stairwell.

The steps led to a landing with two doors, one hung haphazardly off its hinges. Dale righted it and wedged it open before she stepped inside. The wooden floor creaked loudly. The room was dim, and Dale shone her light across the floor before shining it upwards. Large water stains and loose plaster hung from the ceiling.

"What a wreck." Dale photographed the ceiling with her phone and then entered the room. A dirty orange-and-gold couch sat along the north wall next to a brown leather recliner with a torn seat. She moved through the living room to a narrow kitchen that held a two-burner stove.

A window with cracked panes of glass gave view to the alley. A refrigerator stood open, its shelves bare. Just past the kitchen area was a bathroom with a corner sink, a shower, and toilet. The bedroom held a double bed frame and six-drawer chest missing two drawers. The closet door was open to reveal tattered floral wallpaper and rusted wire hangers.

Worn orange shag carpeting covered the floor. Dale mentally added up the cost of reconfiguring the space, as well as cleaning and repairing the kitchen and dining area.

"Are you sure you don't want to demo the whole thing and start over?" Dale scribbled notes on her estimate sheet.

"No. Do you want to see the other apartment? Or is it too big a job for you?" Mai shoved her hands in her pockets.

"Not too big. We can do it. But you're talking a huge investment. At least eight months and that's if the permits go through and without any surprises, like if we run into large amounts of asbestos. Did you have an idea beyond opening up the space of how you want it configured?"

"It needs to be accessible. I have rough sketches and a folder of ideas I've been collecting."

"Send those to me. I can draw up some plans for you to review. All renovations have to be compliant. Did you want to hire an architect? Or designer?"

"Do I need to?"

"No. I can produce plans the city will accept after the city engineer signs off on them."

"Good. That will save money, right?"

"It will." Dale led them back to the apartment kitchen. She opened the cabinets under the sink and shone her flashlight on the plumbing. "Most of this pipe is galvanized and it runs into copper. It's more than likely going to leak like a sieve when we turn the water on. We'll have to tear it all out. Some of the wiring is the original knob and tube, and it will all have to be replaced as well." She glanced at the ceiling. "With all this water damage my guess is the roof is in bad shape. We'll replace that first to give us a dry place to work."

Mai crossed her arms and scowled at Dale. "Is anything salvageable?"

Dale stood up and leaned a hip against the counter. "The bricks are in good shape. The framing seems sound for the most part. And you have some nice fixtures that can be reused." She bent down and flipped back the edge of the rug and pointed to the hardwood floor. "These floors will clean up."

"What about opening the space? My parents made this into two apartments after my grandfather came to live with us." Mai pressed her lips together in a thin line.

Dale pointed to the wall where it joined the ceiling. "If this isn't a supporting wall then it shouldn't be a problem to open it up."

"That's good." Mai walked over to the kitchen area and looked out of the window over the sink. "Downtown has changed a lot. How long will it take before you get me the estimate?"

"It has." Dale tapped her clipboard with her pen. "And I'll need to get up on the roof to look around and take some measurements. And I have to get my roofer out to assess the roof and run my other subcontractors through here. And I'll need to draw up plans for you to approve before I can finish the estimate. Four weeks at the outside, maybe sooner."

Mai tilted her head. "You think I'm crazy? To try to reclaim this?"

"No. Not now. I mean not now that I know who you are."

Mai snorted. "Right. After looking at this I think I'm crazy." She kicked at the rug and flipped it back over the floor. A puff of dirt wafted up.

Dale gripped her clipboard and scribbled Mai's name at the top of her page of notes. "I'll run my plumber and electrician through here this week and get the roofer out as soon as I can. I'll figure cost and materials, write it up, and send it to you. What is the best email for you?"

Mai pulled a silver card case from her front pocket, extracted a card, and held it between two fingers, offering it to Dale. "This my personal contact information. How soon?"

Dale took the card and shoved it under the clip. "It will take at least two weeks to get the estimates from the others. I can start work on the plans as soon as you send me your ideas. Do you have a timeline for when you'd like this completed?"

"As soon as possible." Mai stared at Dale. "Of course."

"Of course." Dale unhooked her tape measure from her belt. "I need to take some measurements. If you have other appointments, you can go. I'll lock up behind me."

Mai crossed her arms over her chest. "I don't have anywhere to be."

*

"I didn't know your name was Dale. Ida never called you anything but Dee." Mai held the end of the tape measure in place.

Dale made a notation on her paper. "I didn't like my name much as a kid."

Mai thought back to the girl Dale had been in high school. She remembered her in short skirts, perfect makeup, and tight blouses displaying a cleavage that left Mai speechless. Dale had been a sophisticated senior when Mai was a scrubby freshman.

She flushed when she remembered her ridiculous attempts to engage Dale when she drove Ida and Mai to basketball practice. The image of Dale Mai remembered bumped up hard against the rough around the edges woman dressed in old jeans and boots who knelt across from her, oblivious to the dirty floor.

"Did you marry that guy? What was his name?"

"Let go now." Dale waited for Mai to release the tape before she pressed the button and rewound it. "Bill. I did."

Mai avoided Dale's eyes, wondering at the clipped tone in her voice. "Kids?"

"Three." Dale's voice warmed and she sat back on her heels. "Boys."

Mai rose and brushed the dust off her pants. "Wow. A house of men."

Dale snorted. "The cat's female for what it's worth." She moved to the large front window. "Help me with this?"

Mai took the end of the tape measure and held it next to the frame.

"Hold it to the inside." Dale held the tape taut as she read the numbers. "Stay there, we'll get the outside measure next." She scratched a note on her estimate sheet.

"Does your Bill work in construction as well?" Mai fiddled with the end of the tape measure as she waited for Dale to finish her note.

"He did."

"What does he do now?"

"Pushes up daisies as far as I know."

Mai frowned. "Sorry?"

"He walked out when my oldest was seven."

Mai sucked in a breath. "I'm sorry. I didn't know."

Dale swept her hair back with her hand and met Mai's gaze. "It's okay. The boys and I are fine. Hold the end to the outside now. Tight to the edge of the sill."

They measured the window in silence. Mai searched for something more to say and failed to come up with anything that didn't sound trite or stupid. Dale went back to work, her face a mask of concentration as she sketched the dining area.

*

The sun was full up when they locked the door to the building. Dale walked ahead of Mai. She stopped at her truck and rested her foot on the bumper, turning her knee into a makeshift desk. She scribbled furiously, her forehead wrinkled as she worked. Her jeans pulled tight across her thick thighs and displayed her ass to perfection. Dale placed the clipboard on the hood of the car. She swiped at her forehead with the back of her wrist before she removed her flannel shirt and hung it on the side mirror.

Mai stared at her smooth skin and well-muscled shoulders. Her gaze wandered over Dale's perfect collarbones and then down to the subtle swell of breasts that pushed against the sides of the tank top. The rib-knit clung to her body and displayed the curve of her hips as it disappeared into her jeans. Dale pulled the shirt free from her jeans and bent to wipe her face.

Mai caught a glimpse of creamy white skin over Dale's hip when she lifted the hem. Dale straightened.

Mai bit her lip and forced herself to look into Dale's eyes. "Um, is there anything else you need from me?"

"No." Dale tapped Mai's business card. "Is the phone number here correct? I'll need to call you to set up the estimates for the plumber and the electrician. Do you have the specs for the kind of cooktops and ovens you want? Do you want the same size walk-in refrigerator and to keep the same configuration for the dishwashing station?"

"Yes." Mai's voice squeaked. "Sorry, yes. The number is correct. And yes. I can email you the specs and my sketches."

Dale picked up her clipboard, pulled a card from under the clip, and passed it to Mai before sweeping her flannel shirt off the side mirror. She hooked it with her finger and draped it over her shoulder. She squared her body to Mai. "Thank you."

Mai frowned. "For what?"

"Not letting me fuck this up and giving me a chance. I was an ass when I showed up. If you decide on me as your contractor, I'll be on time and not be such a jerk."

Mai tilted her head. "We all have bad days. I'm happy you decided to stay."

Dale stepped back. "I'll be in touch." She opened the door and climbed into the truck.

Mai turned and walked to her car. She waited until Dale left the parking lot before she turned and pulled her one suitcase and sleeping bag from the back of her car. She clicked the lock and walked back to the battered door and her new home.

Chapter Two

Dale pulled her truck into a space next to the picnic pavilion of Sikesville's park. The sounds of children squealing and laughing filtered through the trees that blocked the view of the playground. Dale gathered her bulging planner and her lunch cooler before she exited the car.

She brushed the top of the picnic table with her hand before she placed the book on the table. After opening the planner, she dug a sandwich out of the cooler, unwrapped it, and took a bite. *What is wrong with me? I almost walked away from a job.* She flipped through the bills tucked under the flap of the planner and sorted them by due dates and past due dates.

Dale grimaced. *How did it get so bad? Because Molly. And I was stupid enough to believe her lies. Molly. Fuck.* She shook her head to clear the memories of the woman who had cleared out all her money. The empty space Molly left in her bank account was nothing compared to the emptiness in Dale's heart after Molly walked out. *Fuck. Fuck me. Get it together.* She stuffed the bills back into her planner and pulled out her notes from the morning's estimate.

She sipped from her water thermos and listed the subcontractors she would need to do the job. *Mai Li. Why is she here? Ghosts for twenty years and then suddenly reappears?* Curiosity won over work and Dale thumbed on her phone. She typed Mai's name into the search bar.

The first article that came up was a lurid photo of Mai engaged in a shouting match with another woman. The woman was tall and slender and gorgeous. The article was from last year and hidden behind a paywall. The next featured the same photo from a different angle and showed the woman's placid face in contrast to Mai's obvious fury. Dale clicked on it, frustrated as hell when it turned out to be clickbait leading to some ridiculous advertisement for erectile dysfunction drugs.

The next entry listed the canceling of Mai's TV show, *Chefs at Home.* Dale scanned the brief article. *Oh. That's why she has the money to do this. And nowhere to be now.* She finished her sandwich in two bites as she read. Scant on details, the news report hinted Mai and the woman, identified as Charlene Fromer, were more than cohosts and their public spats on and off set had led to the cancellation of the show.

Dale thumbed her phone off. *What do I care? Because she's hot as fuck. And she was kind even when I was a bitch. Was she out in high school? I sure didn't know.* She blew out a breath. *Until it was too late. No, I got my boys out of it. Bill ditching me was the best thing ever happened to us. But damn Molly to hell. Why can't I find a decent person to be with? As lousy at picking women as I was at picking men. Fuck me.* She rested her head on her arms and closed her eyes.

The kind expression on Mai's face when she asked Dale to stay and the way she had looked at her as she apologized rose up in Dale's mind. Another image, the one of Mai's thick shoulders and the way her pants had draped over her sculpted ass, stirred a flush. Dale sat up and pressed her water bottle to her face. Cold condensation trickled down her wrist. *Mai Li. Hot as fuck and out of my league. Not like she'd be interested in a single mom with three kids anyway.*

*

Mai climbed the steps up to the apartments over the restaurant. She kept away from the walls, unwilling to trash her shirt more than she already had. She pulled the wad of keys from her pocket and sorted through them, trying four before she found the right key to open the door. The room was as musty as the other apartment but underlying this one was the faint smell of tobacco. A reminder of the two-pack-a-day habit that had taken her grandfather as it had her father. The apartment was one room, the sole division a small alcove that had been turned into a bathroom and held only a sink and toilet. She turned away and entered her family's apartment.

Memories rushed through her of evenings with her grandfather. Yeye would show up in his plaid flannel robe to shower. After his shower, wrapped in his bathrobe over his striped pajamas, skinny shins sticking out from the hem, he would chain-smoke as he sat with Mai and her sister Yvonne while they did their homework. Even fresh from his shower he always smelled of drugstore cologne, cigarettes, and whiskey.

Mai's mother would bring them food from the restaurant for dinner. Grim faced, she would serve them as her grandfather chided her mother, always finding something to complain about each dish: too hot, too cold, too spicy. His litany of criticism was as much a backdrop to their meals as the hum of the refrigerator in their small kitchen. Mai's mother never responded to him. Her silence as loud as a shout.

At bedtime, Yeye would read to Mai and Yvonne as he sat on a straight-back kitchen chair beside the double bed they shared. Mai closed her eyes as she remembered the gravelly sound of his voice as he read them stories of trickster foxes, snow princesses, and dragons. Mai placed her suitcase on the floor. She walked back to the bedroom, empty except for a stained and torn damp-swollen phonebook. The dank smell of rodent urine wafted from the room. She turned away and walked back to the living room.

In the living room her gut twisted as another memory surfaced. Memories of waking to the sound of loud voices, arguing, her grandfather with her father, about how families should live together. Mai stared out of the window at the yellow painted bricks of the building across the alley. A white plastic bag caught in the wind tumbled between the buildings. As a child she had wondered why her parents had put up the wall. Why couldn't the family live together?

Her mother's sister, Mai's favorite aunt, had finally answered Mai's questions one night over a bottle of dark rum. Her grandfather had disapproved of Mai's mother's mixed-race heritage. He had offered Mai's mother a bribe not to marry his son. Mai chewed her lip, trying to reconcile her version of her doting grandfather with the racist image her aunt had painted.

"You're finally going to get your wish, Yeye," Mai said aloud and grimaced at the echo. She moved her suitcase to the middle of the room and placed her sleeping bag on top of it. She pulled her phone from her pocket and began her list of what she would need to clean the apartment.

*

Glossy brochures glared at Dale from the dining room table. Thomas, ever detail oriented and watchful of money, was bent over them, his head so close to Noah's they almost touched. "It would be at least thirty-three a year without financial aid and that doesn't include room and board."

Noah chewed his lip and looked up at Dale. "Maybe I could get a scholarship? New York's not that far, Mom."

Dale sat back in her chair. "Fill out the paperwork. The worst they can say is no." She reached across the table and touched the back of Noah's hand. "I can't promise anything, Noah, unless this job comes through. Even then, even with a scholarship, we may not be able to afford it."

Noah pursed his lips and gathered up the brochures. "I know. It was an idea. They have some classes at the community college I can sign up for."

Dale pushed her hair back with both hands. "If I get this job, I'm going to need all of you to help with it. The more we do, the more we make."

Noah stood and tucked the brochures into his backpack. His phone beeped. "Gotta go. Chip's on his way." He snagged an apple out of the bowl on the counter before he charged out of the door.

Dale suppressed her sigh as she watched him go. The rain beat a steady drum on the roof and a rumble of thunder rattled the window. A river of rainwater gushed down the alley behind their house. Guilt, heavy and thick, settled over her, an unwelcome cloak of despair. She should have the money to send Noah to school. She would have had the money. She worked her ass off so her kids could have an easier life and then blew it all trusting the wrong person. She lifted her shoulders and let them fall.

No use fretting. Let it go. She poured herself another cup of coffee before she sat at the table.

"Mom?" Thomas scooted his chair over to sit next to Dale. "I've got the numbers if you're ready to plug them into the estimate."

"What would I do without you, Thomas?" She ruffled her middle son's hair.

"Pay a real bookkeeper a fuckton of money." Thomas snorted and turned his laptop toward Dale.

"Language. I'm still your mother." Dale quirked her mouth at him. "And you're right." She studied the quote on the laptop screen. "Looks good. Print it off for me."

Thomas's fingers flew over the keys and the ancient printer wheezed to life on its stand in the corner of the kitchen and startled Olivia, their equally ancient cat, from her nap. Disgruntled, she sat up and settled her baleful stare on them before she jumped to the floor and stalked off.

"Why not email it? Save you time."

Dale rubbed the back of her neck. "I want to deliver this one in person. It's a big number and I don't want her to freak."

Thomas settled back in his chair. "Is she going to flip the property? Start it up and then sell it? We might be able to shave some of the numbers if she does. We can go with lower end materials if she gets nervous."

"Don't know what she's planning. She was pretty cagey about it. Do you have the figures for the bathroom remodel for the Haskins too?"

Thomas hit a few keys and pulled the estimate up. Dale scanned it. "Looks good. Send it."

"Not worried about Mrs. Haskins freaking?" Thomas raised his eyebrow.

"Nah, she's got enough money to wipe her ass with it."

"Mom! Language." Thomas laughed.

Dale stood up and stretched before she plucked the freshly printed pages from the printer. "Did you see Granddad yesterday?"

"Nope. I think he's spending a lot of time over at Ms. Zettler's house." Thomas waggled his eyebrows at his mom. "Lots of time."

Dale rolled her eyes. "Never you mind about your granddad." Dale placed the estimate into her planner. "Do you have something to wear for your aunt's wedding? Noah is sorted. At least it's an outdoor wedding."

Thomas sat back in the chair. "I'm good. Are you?"

Dale tilted her head. "As good as I'm going to be." She grimaced.

"We don't have to go." Thomas met Dale's gaze.

Dale snorted. "We do. I do. Even if I think it's the second stupidest thing your aunt has ever done. At least she divorced George before he spent them into bankruptcy."

Thomas rested his hand on his hips. "Free food and booze. I'll even drive. You can have as much wine as you want."

"You don't have to worry about me, I'm still the mom."

"You are. And I'm not a kid. And not everyone is a con artist. Jeff is a good guy. You need to give him a chance."

Dale swept her hand though her hair. "Why? He doesn't even have a job. He's a bum. He's always been a bum."

"He's got a job lined up. He's kind to Aunt Ida. People change, Mom."

"I'll believe it when I see it." Dale swigged the last of her coffee gone cold while they talked.

*

Mai scrubbed the black-and-white honeycomb floor tiles. Her knees ached. She rinsed the scrub brush and the scent of the ammonia water rose up, comforting her. From twelve on, after Mai's Yeye had died, she and her sister sat in the corner booth every night the restaurant was open. They did their homework in between busing tables and ferrying orders out to tables. The ritual of cleaning the floors of the kitchen after closing was a much a part of her as breathing.

A fat raindrop splattered the floor followed by a dozen more before Mai could rise to her feet and slam the window shut. The thick glass rattled in the frame as the rain beat against it. Mai finished scrubbing the last bit of tile and dumped the water down the bathtub drain. She turned on the tap and rinsed the bucket after letting the rust-colored water clear. She had taken a chance and had the water turned on to the building. She had quickly discovered Dale had been right in her assessment and the pipes under the sink had leaked. Mai had closed off the water in the kitchen. At least the bathroom pipes seemed sound and the toilet, after hours of cleaning, was functional and not too dismal.

She turned the bucket upside down to drain and grimaced at the rust stains and chips in the huge tub. Her phone vibrated, and she dried her hands on her shirt and pulled it from her pocket. A bright-orange weather alert banner scrolled across the screen.

Rain drummed on the roof and the unmistakable sound of running water filled her ears. Mai bolted from the bathroom while shoving her phone into her pants. Water streamed from the ceiling in three places where the plaster ballooned out. Mai dodged the water and bent over to snatch her sleeping bag off the floor.

A large chunk of plaster crashed to the floor and dirty water poured after it. She tossed her shoes into her suitcase, yanked the zipper of her suitcase closed, and ran for the stairs. Water dripped over the steps and soaked into Mai's clothes as she navigated the dark stairwell.

At the bottom of the stairs, Mai patted her pockets for her keys. A crack of thunder shook the building. No keys. Mai cursed. She tossed her sleeping bag and suitcase to the floor and took the stairs two at a time. She skidded to a stop at the doorway. Most of the ceiling lay in large chunks on the floor and through the now open ceiling, she could see dark dangerous clouds. A flash of lightning lit the room.

Mai dashed across the floor, scooped her keys up off the countertop, and fled. Her wet feet slipped on the steps and she fell the last four steps and landed on her sleeping bag and suitcase. The handle of her bag dug into her ribs and she dropped her keys. Biting back her scream, she scrambled to her feet. She moved her now sopping wet sleeping bag as she searched for her keys with trembling hands.

Another crash of thunder rattled the building. Mai scrabbled with her hands and came up empty. She sat back on her heels, her breathing harsh in the closed space of the landing. A steady flow of water down the steps wet her jeans and reminded her she couldn't stay where she was. The yellow glint of the happy face emoji on her key ring shone on the dark floor. The keys were lying on the floor of the kitchen. Mai snatched her bag off the landing, stopped long enough to scoop her keys off the floor, and ran for the back door.

Sharp stones dug into her bare feet as she dashed toward her car while pushing the unlock button. Mai yanked the door open, tossed her suitcase into the passenger seat, and clambered into the car. Wet and shivering, she jammed the key into the ignition and started the car.

Cool air blasted her from the vents, and she turned the temperature control to heat. The air in the car became warm and the windows fogged. Mai pulled her phone from her damp pocket and prayed the case had kept it dry. She thumbed on the screen and opened the weather app. Dark bands of red filled the radar screen.

Gravel pelted her door and bounced off the window as a gust of wind rocked the car. Sheets of rain made it impossible to see across the parking lot. Mai opened her bag, grateful when she touched dry clothes. She stripped off her T-shirt and tossed it onto the floorboard.

Shivering, she tugged a clean dry shirt over her head. Navigating the steering wheel while she grappled with her wet jeans and underwear had her sweating and cursing. Her jeans and briefs joined the shirt on the car mat. With more wiggling she managed to pull on a pair of soft sweatpants.

Mai leaned her head on the steering wheel. The car warmed and Mai stopped shivering. She eyed the gas gauge and turned the car off, cursing herself for letting it get low. She pushed her wet hair out of her eyes and pulled the lever and lowered the seat back.

She stretched out and pulled her coat from the back seat and pulled it over her. Unwilling to risk driving in the storm, she closed her eyes and let the sound of the rain pounding on the roof lull her to sleep.

Chapter Three

Dale drove over a small tree limb and assorted debris as she pulled in the parking lot, proud of herself for arriving early. Pricked by memories of their last meeting, she had woken early, showered, and taken some time to find her good jeans and wear a newish V-neck T-shirt that displayed her assets. She had even spent some time with her hair and thrown on a bit of concealer and lip gloss.

She ignored the churning in her stomach at the thought of seeing Mai again. *It's because this job is important.* A wave of guilt surged through her. *Like lip gloss will get her to sign the contract.* She smiled to herself at the thought of beating Mai to their appointment as she imagined the look on Mai's face. *No use not using what I have.* Her grin faded and she snorted when she saw Mai's car. *Not early enough. For fuck's sake.*

After parking the truck next to the car, movement in the car drew her attention and she peered down. Long shapely legs leading up to bright-blue briefs filled her vision and then were blocked from her sight as Mai's naked back, her lean muscles flexing as she struggled to pull her jeans up in the confines of the car, filled Dale's vision. When Mai sat up and leaned back to button her jeans her breasts came into view. Dale's breath caught and she looked away from her small, perfectly shaped breasts tipped with dark-brown nipples.

A warm flush crept up Dale's face and her nipples peaked against the fabric of her bra. *What the hell is wrong with me? She's a client. What's she doing changing in her car? Her back. Get it together. This is business. Business.*

Dale waited a beat before she opened her door and climbed down from the truck. She leaned against the door to give Mai privacy to complete dressing. A breeze, a gift from the storm last night, filtered through the trees. She closed her eyes and lifted her hair off her neck in an effort to cool down.

"Dale?"

Mai's voice, much too close, startled her. She opened her eyes and peered into Mai's face. "Hi." Dale's voice rasped and she cleared her throat. "I've got your quote. I was thinking I would be early. But I think I'd have to sleep here to get here before you."

Mai covered her yawn. "I don't recommend it." She rubbed the back of her neck.

Dale frowned at her. "Wait, what? Did you sleep here? What's wrong with you? The building is unsafe, at least until we get the roof fixed."

Mai stepped back. "I didn't sleep in there last night." She looked away from Dale's eyes.

Dale caught the evasion in Mai's voice. "But you've been sleeping here?" She placed her hand on her hip. "Why? You broke?"

Mai squared herself and met Dale's hard-edged glare. "No. I don't like wasting money. I had a place to stay. This was my home once upon a time. Why would I stay in a hotel? It adds up, you know."

Dale swept her hand through her hair. "Fine. Whatever. You want to sleep someplace the roof can come down on your head at any moment suit yourself." She shoved the estimate folder at her. "Here's your estimate."

Mai took the folder from Dale and tucked it under her arm. "Do you want to go somewhere and get coffee?"

Dale cocked her head to the side. "Is this your way of telling me I'm being an ass again?"

Mai failed to stifle a yawn. "No. I didn't sleep well last night. I need some myself."

Dale rested her one hand on her hip. "Did you sleep in your car?"

Mai's sheepish grin stirred Dale. "Yes."

Dale's face burned as she pushed away images of her glimpse of a near-naked Mai. "Bella's shop is around the corner. If you don't mind the smell of hipster beard oil and a bunch of college kids, it's decent coffee and we can walk to it."

Dale looked up at the building. "How bad did it get last night you slept in the car?"

"Let's say you're probably going to have to add to your estimate."

Dale arched her eyebrow.

Mai rubbed the back of her neck. "Most of the apartment ceiling is on the floor and there is a hole in the roof the size of a couch."

"For fuck's sake, Mai, you could have been killed." Dale's stomach clenched.

"I know. I know now. Can we go get coffee? I don't need you telling me how much of an idiot I am. I feel stupid enough as it is." Mai's dark eyes glittered, and her mouth set in a thin line.

Dale sucked in a breath before she spoke. "Sorry. Yeah. Let's go."

*

Women with toddlers in their laps sat thigh to thigh with hipsters decked out in flannel. College students gulped their coffee as they worked on laptops and benches provided most of the seating at the wide board tables.

Mai pointed to a table for two next to the window at the front of the cafe. "Why don't you grab us a seat? How do you like your coffee?"

"Black, please, medium roast."

Mai lifted her eyebrow. "They have different roasts here?"

Dale squinted at Mai. "They do. We're not that backwater."

Mai dug in the pocket of her pants. No wallet. She patted her other pockets. She flushed, her cheeks on fire. *Fucking great. Ask her to coffee and then don't have any money.* She rubbed the back of her neck. "Um. I'm sorry. I don't have my wallet on me." The mad scramble of last evening came back to her. *Did I even grab it? Where the hell is it?* She scrubbed her hand over her face. "I'll go back. I think it's in my car."

Dale lifted her chin. "It's fine. Go get the table so we can hear ourselves."

Mai slouched toward the table. *When did it all go sideways? What the fuck am I doing?* She glanced out of the window at the row of small business storefronts across the street from the shop. Some of the stores had the same signs she remembered from growing up. Others boasted new signs and businesses. A clothing boutique shared a wall with a cooking store directly across the street from the coffee shop. Johnson's shoe store and leather repair shop, a relic from Mai's childhood, stood on the corner. A red neon light advertising Red Wing boots glowed next to a green "open" sign.

Dale placed a bowl-sized mug of coffee in front of her. "You look like you needed a large one."

Mai grimaced. "I'd drink right from the carafe this morning." She placed the blue folder squarely on the table between them and rested her hand on top of it.

"Before you look at the final number, remember we can use less expensive materials. I costed the job using medium grade materials for everything. It will give us a starting point."

Dale's gaze was intense, her blue eyes dark, and Mai studied them. She heard her father's voice in her head. *It's in their eyes, Mai. If you look hard enough you can see right into someone's soul. Always look in their eyes when doing business.* Mai sat back in her chair and lifted her coffee. She held Dale's gaze over the rim as she sipped the hot brew. *She needs this job. Wants it bad enough to deliver the estimate herself.*

Mai swallowed and the smooth flavor of the coffee filled her mouth. "This is glorious."

"They roast it themselves. And don't act so surprised."

Mai dragged the file folder to her side of the table and opened it. She fought her urge to squirm under Dale's direct gaze. Flipping the pages quickly, she got to the final cost. *Enough. I have enough. But will I after last night? Stupid storm.* "This will increase with what happened last night, correct?"

Dale frowned. "It may, if there was extensive water damage. I won't know if it will or by how much until I check out the building." She rubbed her finger over the edge of her cup. "You can't sleep there. Not now. The whole roof could collapse." She reached across the table and rested her fingertips on the back of Mai's hand. "Please tell me you won't."

Mai's skin burned with Dale's touch and her stomach clenched. She yanked her hand away. "Umm. Okay." Her shoulders slumped. "I don't know if I'll have enough to do this."

Dale leaned back in her chair and placed her hands flat on the table. "Can you borrow it?"

Mai's head lifted her head. "I won't. I would have had the cash to do everything. Now I'm not sure."

Dale knotted her hands together. "You were going to have to replace the roof anyway. When will you decide? Are you going to walk away?"

Mai rolled the cup between her hands. "No. I'll figure it out."

Dale pursed her lips. "Whatever you decide, you need someone to take a look at the roof and tarp it, so you don't have any more water damage."

"You think I'm stupid to do this, to try to open a restaurant here, don't you?"

Dale shrugged. "Everyone has their reasons for doing anything. I'm not judging you."

Mai snorted. "I think I'm beyond stupid." She gestured across the street to the shoe shop. "I want to have my own business. A place for Yvonne and me to live. Nothing fancy. A life of making food that makes folks happy. Like my parents had."

Dale's gaze pinned her in place. "Every time women step out and do something different folks say you're crazy. You should've heard the things people said to me when I moved back here after Bill left us. And then they doubled down on the assholishness after I started my contracting business. Bill might have been a jerk, but I learned a lot from him about contracting. Most of the established subcontractors wouldn't work with me. I found other women in the trades to work with. Most of us have been where you are. We can work on the financing. Don't let jackasses who will spend their lives building someone else's dream tell you that you can't build yours."

*

The deep shadows under Mai's eyes tugged at Dale's heart. *Who's Yvonne? Doesn't matter. So afraid to spend money she slept in her car. At least she didn't have to figure out how to sleep in a car with three kids.*

Mai lowered her forehead to the tabletop.

Dale reached over and patted her shoulder, her fingers lingering on the tight muscles under her thin shirt. The sensation sparked want, low in her belly, and her fingers trembled. *Wow. Lots of time in the gym. Get it together. She's not on the market. Lucky Yvonne.* "Hey. Look at me."

Mai lifted her head. Her dark eyes shimmered.

"Why don't we go back and get your car? I have a spare room. You can stay there."

Mai lifted an eyebrow. "I haven't made a decision about the project. I don't want to take advantage of you."

Dale snorted. "I'm not worried about it. Even if you don't say yes to me doing the work, you need a place to sleep. Women with dreams need to stick together." She stood up and drained her coffee cup. "Come on. Before the after-yoga rush makes it impossible to get out the door."

Chapter Four

Dale led the way down a narrow set of steps to the basement. She pointed at a white four-panel door. "Washer and dryer's through there if you need it."

They walked past a weight bench and a bin of ball bats, hockey sticks, and various sports balls before stopping outside a door painted a lurid shade of green. Dale opened the door and flipped a light switch.

A musty smell greeted them. In the middle of the floor was a thin mattress on a low frame. Worn carpet, the threads showing through in places, covered the floor. Under the basement window was a squat black chest of drawers.

Mai set her suitcase on the floor. She chewed her lip and pondered how to say she would rather sleep in her car. *Don't be an idiot. Say thank you. You'd be dry and safe.*

Dale rested her hands on her hips. "It'll be better once we air it out. I haven't been in here since Seth moved in with his girlfriend."

"Seth?"

"My oldest. You spoke with him on the phone." Dale sighed and turned away. With a forceful shove she opened the window over the dresser. "This should help." She frowned at Mai. "You seem underwhelmed."

Mai barked a laugh. "Sorry. My mother raised me better. Thank you."

"I've got a pillow and some sheets for the futon somewhere upstairs. I'll bring them down."

She walked out of the door, the set of her shoulders somewhere between pissed off and sad.

Mai left her bag by the door. "Hey, Dale?"

Dale stopped and turned to Mai. In the dim light Mai could barely see her eyes. "I'm grateful. I was freaked out last night. I hardly slept. Thank you for opening your home to me. I don't know how to repay you."

Dale's eyes gleamed in the dim light. "Mm, yes, well I have some ideas."

Mai sucked in a breath. *Flirting? Is she flirting? Is she trying to seduce me into hiring her? No. Stop it, Mai. She's not like that. This is not LA.*

A hint of a smile played around Dale's mouth. "Come upstairs and let's talk."

Mai looked down at the steps and counted them on the way back up to the kitchen to keep from staring at Dale's magnificent ass, trying to stem the lurid images of what she could do to pay Dale back for giving her a place to sleep.

Dale sat down at the cluttered dining room table and pointed to the chair opposite her.

Mai pulled the chair out and sat.

Dale grabbed a glossy brochure off the sideboard. "It's like this." She tapped a short nail on the cover. "My Noah wants to go to culinary school."

Mai rested her hands on the edge of the table. "And?"

"And I'm helping Thomas with his college accounting classes right now, and even if I wasn't, I can't afford to send Noah away to school."

Mai frowned. "Is this a way to get me to say yes? Guilt me into it?"

Dale stood up and raked her hand through her hair. "No. No matter what you decide about the renovation, you're going to need a place to live, right? And you don't want to dip into your building fund, right? How about room and board in exchange for you teaching Noah?"

Mai sat back in her chair. "I'm not a professional teacher. The show was scripted."

Dale raised her eyebrow. "You grew up in your parents' kitchen, you've worked in kitchens your entire life—for fuck's sake don't you think you could at least teach a high school kid how to cook?"

Mai drummed her fingers on the table. "What about the job? What if I choose another contractor?"

Dale tilted her head and skewered Mai with her glare. "You think I don't know the other contractors in this town? I know you haven't even had anyone else look at it. If this was some silly thing where you're not sure you're even going to do this project say it now. You're still welcome to stay because I don't want to think about you sleeping in that death trap. But if you're serious, I'm willing to work with you on the costs."

Mai raised her gaze to Dale's stormy blue eyes. "Okay."

Dale held out her hand and Mai shook it.

Dale rubbed her thumb over the back of Mai's hand. "At least I know I'll get something wonderful to eat out of our bargain." She held on to Mai's hand a moment longer and then a tinge of pink colored her cheeks. She yanked her hand away. "I just—I'll go find those sheets. Make yourself at home."

She retreated from the kitchen and Mai glanced around at the chaos and cluttered countertops. *Why the hell did I say yes? What the hell do I know about teaching a high school boy to cook?*

*

The sharp buzz of a phone call made Dale pat her pockets. *Not mine.* Mai's voice filtered through the hall as Dale dug through the hallway closet and the ramshackle stacks of mismatched sheets. She tugged a rumpled stack of plum-colored sheets from the closet and tucked them under her arm along with a bright-blue pillowcase.

Mai's bright laugh and conspiratorial tone made Dale clench her jaw. *Must be Yvonne. Wonder when she'll show up.* Dale quirked her mouth and shook her head to clear her annoyance over how happy Mai sounded. *So what? They're happy. Good. I should be happy for her.* She hurried to her bedroom and snatched a pillow off her bed. *Quilt. She's going to need a quilt.*

Dale left the stack of linens on the bed. She opened the chest at the foot of her bed. The scent of cedar rushed out to greet her and she lifted a crocheted blanket from the pile and then added a Toy Story print comforter to the pile. After gathering all of the bedclothes in her arms she walked back to the kitchen.

"I love you. I'll talk to you next week." Mai turned toward Dale as she pocketed her phone. "Let me help you." Mai grabbed the blankets and the pillow from Dale.

"Thanks." Dale hated how clipped her tone sounded.

Mai's brows drew down and shadowed her eyes. "Are you sure you're okay with this."

"Why would I offer if I wasn't?"

Mai shrugged. "Because you're feeling sorry for me? I don't know."

Dale turned away from Mai. "I don't say things I don't mean. Not anymore." She walked to the steps leading to the basement. "Let's get your bed made. I have an appointment I need to get to."

*

"I can't believe you're going to stay with us." Noah hurried down the stairs behind Mai, carrying her duffel bag.

Mai stopped at the bottom of the stairs. "Me either. Thanks for helping me."

Noah placed her suitcase on the edge of the rug.

Mai held up her sleeping bag, grimacing at the musty smell. *Should have laid it out to dry.* She held it at arm's length. "I need to wash this."

"Lemme show you where the washer is."

Mai followed Noah to the laundry room. She stepped over a pile of clothes on the floor. "I don't want to disrupt laundry day."

Noah snorted. "Every day is laundry day. It's fine. I'm so behind it won't make any difference." He opened the lid of the washer. "There's soap and you might want to put some vinegar in with it. I use it on Mom's work clothes."

Mai loaded her sleeping bag into the washer. "You do the laundry?"

Noah shifted his feet. "Yeah. It helps Mom. She works hard enough as it is."

"That's good. Some kids go to college and don't even know how to use a washer."

Noah pressed his lips in a thin line. "At least they get to go."

Mai tilted her head to look into his eyes. "Hey. There are lots of ways to get to college."

Noah nodded. "It'd help if I had better grades."

Mai winced at the shame in his voice. "Grades aren't everything, Noah. Come on, let's check out your kitchen."

*

The kitchen counters were crowded with papers, appliances, and a basket of spotty bananas. The sink overflowed with an array of dirty plates and silverware. An unwashed empty coffee press perched on a cutting board next to the oven. Pots, both clean and unwashed, sat atop the stove. Mai blew out a breath.

Noah's cheeks flamed red. "Um, I would have cleaned up if I had known you were going to be here."

"It's a good place to start. Rule number one. Clean as you go." Mai moved the dishes out of the sink and piled them on the counter. "You have a dishwasher?"

"Yeah." Noah gestured to the closed door of an under-cabinet dishwasher. "It doesn't work." He shoved his hands in his pockets. "It hasn't worked in a while."

Mai opened the door and pulled out the racks. "Okay, then we'll use it as a dish drainer. Where is your dish soap?" She rummaged in the cabinet under the sink.

"It's on top." Noah came and stood next to Mai. He reached over the pile of dishes and retrieved the bottle of blue liquid soap.

Mai filled the sink with hot water and added a squirt of soap. "Now in the kitchen there is a right way to do everything." A flash of her mother standing next to her as Mai stood on a step stool to help wash dishes in their restaurant bubbled up and she shook her head to stave off her melancholy. Nineteen years on and she still missed her mom.

She plucked a glass from the collection of dishes. "Work from lightly clean to the dirtiest. Glasses first, then silverware, plates, followed by pots and pans. Air dry is best if you've got the time and space. Get a clean towel. You dry and then you can show me where things are stored."

Noah opened a drawer and pulled a worn terry cloth dish towel from a stack. "I'm ready."

They worked in silence for a few minutes. Noah dried the glasses before storing them.

"What's it like to have a cooking show?" Noah opened the drawer and sorted the silverware into the appropriate slots in the holder.

Mai swiped the dishcloth over the plate she was washing. "It's exhilarating. And exhausting. And fun as hell."

"It must have sucked when they canceled it." Noah's refreshing adolescent bluntness made Mai chuckle.

"It sure did. Out loud even."

Noah guffawed. "Mom would yell at me for saying 'sucked.'"

Mai raised her eyebrows. "Your mom swears like a trooper."

"I know, right? But she wants us not to."

"I guess it's a mom thing."

"One time, in fourth grade, I had to do a book report. I hated the book and at the end of my report I wrote 'this book really sucks.'"

Mai laughed. "What happened?"

"Mom and I had to go to school to talk to my teacher. I was freaked out. Mom told the teacher she agreed with me, the book did suck, but she'd encourage me to expand my vocabulary."

Mai laughed harder. "I bet that was not what the teacher was expecting."

Noah grinned. "No, it was not."

Mai moved on to the pots. The dried-on remains of soup clung stubbornly to the side of a pot. "I'm going to let this soak."

Noah draped the dish towel over his shoulder. "Now what?"

"Now we clear the decks. Anything not related to food and cooking on the counter needs to find another place to be." She pointed at the cat on the bar that separated the kitchen from the dining room, nestled on a flannel shirt she recognized as Dale's. "What about her?"

Noah shrugged. "She'll pretty much sleep wherever Mom's stuff is." With one hand he lifted the cat and drew her to his chest as he picked up the shirt. He carried the cat gently to the dining room table. He placed the shirt in a chair and then placed the cat on top of it. The cat glared at Noah before yawning. She meowed sharply and circled three times before she lay down on the shirt.

Chapter Five

"I had a look at the roof and the storm damage. I've added the costs to the original estimate." Dale tapped the bottom row of figures. "This is the final projected costs." She leaned back in her chair and rested her hands flat on the table. "It could go up if we get into the renovation and discover structural weakness. Or more asbestos." She grimaced. "That would drive up costs significantly."

Mai fiddled with her pen, spinning it in a circle on the table as she studied the page in front of her. Dale sipped her coffee.

Mai raised her head and met Dale's gaze and picked up the pen. "I'm committed to this." She pointed the pen tip at Dale. "How much to start work?" She signed the contract with a flourish before passing the pen to Dale.

The scent of Mai's cologne, citrus and sandalwood, wove its way into Dale's brain and her resolve to stick to business melted with Mai's nearness. She stared into Mai's dark eyes, drawn to their inky depths. Dale gripped the edge of the table to keep from leaning closer, even as her whole body screamed for her to find out if Mai's lips were as soft as they looked. A flare of desire crossed Mai's features and disappeared so fast Dale almost believed she had not seen it.

"With folks I know, I don't charge anything to start on small jobs. Even on large jobs, I never ask for more than a quarter of the estimate to start. So, a quarter to start will be fine." Dale pulled the contract toward her and signed on the line with her name on it. "Because you want to be green and reuse materials as much as possible, I'll make use of our local Habitat for Humanity ReStore building supplies store. That should help decrease costs in line with what we've discussed. I'll reuse as many materials as we can. Restaurants are the most frequent business fails, so we should be able to pick up used equipment for the kitchen which will save costs. I've already asked my friends to start saving their wine bottles." She smirked at Mai.

Mai rolled her eyes. "It's a solid design. I'll have to get a counter check. I don't have a checkbook."

"No rush on the deposit. It's not like I don't know where you live." Dale picked up the stack of papers and tapped them on the table to square them before she tucked them back into the bright-blue folder.

"When will you start?" Mai rubbed the back of her neck.

Dale stood and placed her chair under the table. "I've got the roofer scheduled to start in three weeks. Weather permitting."

Mai frowned. "Pretty cocky. You didn't even know if I'd sign." She crossed her arms over her chest. "Why so long? Isn't there something you could do before? Why can't you start before the roofer? I want this done as soon as possible."

"Most people do. Things have to be done safely and in the proper order and permits need to be obtained." Dale's jaw clenched and she looked at the ceiling before she brought her gaze back to Mai's face. "We won't start anything until the roof is repaired and I've made sure the building is safe. I'm not going to risk my crew for whatever timeline you've imagined. You're very lucky Alex, the building inspector, is busy. He would have yellow taped the place the morning after the storm."

"What about another roofer?"

"No. Gloria is the best. She has the best prices and does the best work here. And she is busy as hell this time of year. If she didn't owe me a favor it would have been at least eight weeks before we could start. And it will take me at least four weeks to get all the permits, and we're not starting without them. It's not my first time at the rodeo."

Mai shifted her stance and opened her mouth to speak.

Stepping into her space, Dale held up her hand palm forward. "Look, I'll make you a deal. I won't tell you how to cook and you don't tell me how to run this project." The scent of Mai's cologne made Dale sway closer, and her anger melted with Mai's nearness.

"Sorry." Mai uncrossed her arms, stepped back, and ran her hand through her hair. "Deal. I'll go to the bank this afternoon." She jammed her hands into her jean pockets before she turned and walked swiftly to the basement stairs.

Dale tapped the folder with the signed contract against her leg. Mai's shoulders were rigid, her posture stiff. Dale opened her mouth to call her back, to spend a few more minutes absorbing her delicious scent, to voice an apology, to say anything that would bring Mai back to the table, and let Dale spend a few more minutes lost in her dreamy dark eyes. She cursed herself for letting her anger spoil a moment between them. Again.

Chapter Six

Noah parked the truck a few blocks from the cordoned-off streets that marked the boundaries of the farmer's market. The streets were already busy with folks waiting for the opening bell to signal the start of the market.

"Got our list?" Mai sipped from her thermal coffee mug.

Noah flipped his spiral notebook open and unclipped a pen from his shirt. "Right here."

"Buying produce is a tricky thing. You want the freshest you can get for the best tasting food." She unbuckled her seat belt and lifted the collection of canvas shopping bags from the plastic basket behind her seat. Balancing her coffee cup and the bags, she exited the truck.

"Once the chicken bell rings, we can start buying stuff."

"What?"

Noah pointed at a large brass bell mounted on a post. The image of a rooster was embossed on the side of the bell. "The rooster bell. It's so folks don't start pressuring the sellers to start early." He gestured toward a low row of tables covered by a bright-green popup tent. "Sally's Fresh Produce" was printed in red block letters on a white sign suspended below the tent on one end. "That's Chip's family's stall. They grow organic as much as they can. His mom works with the folks at the agricultural extension on integrated pest management."

Mai followed the line of Noah's gaze.

A blush spread across his cheeks as his gaze settled on a brown-skinned boy with short jet-black hair stacking crates of produce behind the table. "There's Chip. Come on."

Noah led the way and Mai followed him through the crowd. The sharp clang of the bell sounded, and the low buzz of the crowd became louder as people began to make their transactions.

"Hey Chip, I brought Mai."

Chip held out his hand across the table. "Hi."

Mai shook his hand. "Nice to meet you. You grow all this?" Mai looked down the wide selection of lettuces and heirloom vegetables.

"Yeah. My mom and me. And my sisters."

"Chip, keep up, Mr. Jenkins is staring holes in you. Go ring his order." A tall woman with umber skin, her natural curls held back with a dark-green hair band, tapped Chip on the shoulder.

"On it." Chip ducked his head and trotted to the far end of the table. Noah followed as if on a string. Mai studied Noah as he talked to Chip between customers.

"I'm Sally. Are you the famous Mai? Noah has bent my ear every day on the way to cross-country practice about you."

"I don't know about famous, but I am Mai. And nice to meet you, Sally. Your produce is gorgeous. Do you supply any of the restaurants here?"

Sally frowned. "No. Most of the restaurants here are chains. All their business is contracted to big suppliers. I do this market, and the one in Camden in the middle of the week."

"I'm opening a restaurant here, most likely next fall. I want to do a farm-to-table kind of thing. Would you be interested?"

Sally glanced down the now crowded table. "I might be. We'd need to talk some about it. Noah's got my number, have him give it to you. Even if we don't do business, the boys are best friends. Why don't you and Dale come over some night? We can chill with some wine while they watch those god-awful horror movies they like."

"Oh, well. Dale and I aren't... We aren't... I just live there."

Sally raised an eyebrow. "Oh? Well, you're certainly welcome to come by yourself, if you want. Anytime."

"Mom! Do you have Ms. Walker's bushel of tomatoes set aside? She's here to pick them up."

"Under the center table, Chip. Got to go. Nice meeting you." Sally hurried to Chip's side.

Mai pondered Sally's invitation and her assumption that she and Dale were a couple. A couple with an instant family. Mai watched as Sally and Chip worked together, their bond so strong it was palpable. Family. Mai chewed her lip, stunned by how much envy flared in her chest.

She'd never wanted to give birth to kids, but she had wanted to be a parent. Charlene had laughed in her face when she had suggested it. *No. Not destined be a parent. Can't assume that role. I'm Noah's friend. Role model. A queer aunty.*

Noah touched Mai's elbow. "You want to show me how to pick the best stuff?"

"Sure." Mai looped their collection of bags over her arm and they started down the table. They stopped at each item they needed for the meals they had planned for the week. Noah picked up the items Mai chose and placed them in the bag. At the end of the row of tables, Chip added up their purchases. Noah paid for everything from the envelope of cash Dale had left with him.

The small hairs on the back of Mai's neck prickled to attention. The sensation of being watched settled over her. She lifted on her toes to see over the heads of the crowd. A burly blonde security guard was standing at the edge of the crowd. Her dark eyes set in her pasty white face settled on Mai. Her broad hands rested on her wide leather belt loaded with equipment.

"Noah, what's up with the security guard?" Mai inclined her head toward the woman.

Noah glanced in the direction Mai had indicated. "You wouldn't believe it, but some folks shoplift at the market."

"Bad enough you need security?"

Noah shrugged. "Town council thought we did."

The woman shifted her gaze to Noah and then back to Mai.

"Why the hell is she looking at us like that?"

Noah blushed. "Um. She and Mom used to date. But they broke up. And she's still sorta mad about it."

Mai stifled a grin. "Guess she thinks I'm dating your mom, or something."

Noah laughed. "Or something."

Noah's gaze trailed back to Chip and settled there.

Mai rested her hand on his shoulder. "You like Chip."

Noah turned to her. "Yeah. He's my best friend." A blush colored his cheeks.

"You like *like* him." Mai squeezed his shoulder.

Noah lowered his chin to his chest and peered at her from under his bangs. "It doesn't matter. I don't think he likes me the same way."

Mai turned them toward a stall selling baked goods. "I'm not sure about that. Does anyone but me know?"

"No. I don't want Mom to worry." Noah lifted his gaze to Mai's face. "Guys like me get beat up a lot here."

Mai pursed her lips. "I won't say anything. But at some point, you need to tell her. She'll handle it. Better than you think, I bet. What's the story with Chip's mom?"

"She's cool. Bi, I think. Why? You want to date her?"

"Good lord, Noah. I'm not interested in dating right now. Why are you such a little matchmaker?"

Noah frowned. "Because of Yvonne? Are you going to get married to her?"

"What? No! Yvonne is my sister. Why'd you think she was my girlfriend?"

"Your sister? Wow. Cool."

Mai glared at Noah. "Why is that cool?"

Noah's eyes gleamed. "Because it is."

Mai rolled her eyes at him and tugged at his sleeve. "Come on, Yenta, we need to buy bread."

"We're not going to make it ourselves?"

"In the future, yes, but we today we have too many other things to focus on."

They purchased a loaf of crusty olive bread and some rolls for breakfast. Mai's stomach rumbled. They sat on a bench and opened the bag of rolls. She pulled apart a roll and offered half to Noah.

Opposite the bench was a large display of dahlias. Vivid yellow and golds mixed with magenta and rust-colored blooms as they exploded from lush greenery.

Mai stood and stretched. "Have we everything on our list?"

Noah shoved the last of his roll in his mouth and pulled the notebook from his bag. He tapped the tip of the pen against his lip as he studied the list. "Yep."

"I'm going to get some flowers for the table."

Noah frowned. "I don't think Mom would want me to spend money on flowers."

"This is my purchase." She picked up her bags. "Come on. Then we'll go home and work on your knife skills."

*

"I haven't flown a kite in years." Mai tugged gently on the string, thrilled by the answering pull as the kite rose on the strong wind off the lake.

Noah pointed to the small purple dot of the kite in the sky. "You've really got it up there. We've got more line in the truck if we need it."

Mai rubbed her thumb over the custom hardwood line holder. Intricate inlays decorated the handle. It was polished smooth and had the patina time added to any well-loved bit of wood. "How much is on here?"

"Five hundred feet." Wind gusted over the lake, stirring small white caps. Dale zipped up her hooded sweatshirt.

"Mom made it extra big." The pride in Noah's voice made Mai smile.

Mai let out the string as the kite rose higher. "When I was little, Yeye, my grandpa, would take us up to the kite festival in Cleveland. You ever been?"

"No. But it sounds like fun." Dale shaded her eyes with her hand. "When is it?"

"Late summer, I think. It was always right before we went back to school, like August."

Noah held a football up and waved it. "Go long, Mom."

Dale turned and sprinted down the sand at the edge of the lake. Noah lobbed a wobbly spiral at her and she jumped, caught it, clutched it tight to her chest, and promptly wiped out. She lay there a second before she lifted the football in triumph and scrambled to her feet.

Mai laughed. "The Browns could use you!"

Noah pumped his fist. "Way to go, Mom!"

"Noah!" Chip's voice carried over the wind as he jogged toward Noah.

Dale handed the football to Noah. "Go on."

Noah ducked his head, took the football from his mom, and loped toward Chip.

"Chip seems like a decent kid." Mai stepped to the left and let out some more string. The kite dipped and then rose again, the string pulling tight.

Dale shaded her eyes and watched the boys as they ran down the beach, tossing the football back and forth. "Uh huh."

Mai chewed her lip. *Does she know? See how much he's infatuated by Chip? Get it about her son?*

Dale gestured at the kite. "It'll take a least an hour to get it down."

"You in a hurry?" Mai tilted her head at Dale.

Dale drummed her fingers on her knee. "No." She glanced down the beach. The boys were walking now, close to each other, their heads almost touching as they strolled along the sand.

"You worried about Noah and Chip? Not much trouble they can get into here." Mai gestured to the shore. One other group at the far end of the beach was their only company.

"There is more than one kind of trouble." Dale sat down where the grass gave way to the beach and lifted a hand full of sand and let it run between her fingers.

Mai carefully let out enough string to enable her to sit next to Dale. "I hear worry in your voice."

Dale glanced at Mai. "Isn't that what parents are supposed to do? Worry about their kids?"

"Yeah. I guess. I haven't been a parent." Mai shoved the bitter arguments she'd had with Charlene about having a family to the back of her mind. *Too late now. At least I didn't have to navigate an ugly divorce with a kid.* "Noah's smart. He's one of the most mature seventeen-year-olds I've ever met. You've raised an amazing young man."

Dale wiped her hand on her pants leg. "Thanks. But it's not his head I'm worried about."

Unwilling to break Noah's confidence, Mai stayed quiet and fiddled with the kite string.

"I'm not as blind as Noah thinks I am. I know he's interested in Chip, as more than a friend."

"And what's wrong with that?" Mai frowned at Dale.

"Nothing. If Chip feels the same. But in this community, all it would take would be for Noah to indicate his feelings to Chip, have Chip not feel the same, and then he would be outed. Or worse." Dale grimaced.

"Been there done that?" Mai studied Dale's reaction.

"I was grown when I came out. How about you?"

"I knew in high school. Never did anything about it until after graduation."

"I'm a grown woman and when I came out it was still nasty. He's got another year in high school. I'd like him to graduate without having to deal with the ramifications of being out in a small town."

"Is it as bad as when we were growing up?" Mai chewed her lip. "It seems like folks accept you. I've gotten some hard looks, but I never know if it's because folks are racist, or homophobic, or both."

Dale rested her hands on her knees. "It's better. It's safer in some parts of town than others. Where we live, by the college, it's pretty safe and folks are accepting. When you get away from town it can feel unsafe. I wish Noah would talk to me. He used to talk to me about everything. It's not like I wouldn't understand." She picked out a small stone from the sand and flung it toward the lake.

"He'll tell you. He's got to work it out. Maybe he's worried you'll worry more." Mai stood up and began the process of winding the kite in.

"Like a dog chasing its tail. I'm worried about him, and he's worried about me, doesn't talk to me about anything important in his life, and then I worry more." Dale stood and closed the distance between them, close enough their shoulders brushed. "You're good for him. He respects you. He likes you. I know he talks to you."

Mai stood and unwrapped another loop of string from the winder. "Thank you. And I hope it's okay."

Dale rested her hand on Mai's shoulder. "If he's not going to talk to me, I'm more than okay he talks to you. I trust you, Mai. I wouldn't have invited you into my home or let you be around my kid if I didn't."

Mai turned to look into Dale's eyes and was stunned by the warmth of their golden-brown depths. "Thanks for listening." Dale moved her arm and hugged Mai, a quick hug, but the fleeting contact with Dale's body set her aflame.

Mai looped her arm around Dale's waist and hugged her back. "Anytime."

Raucous laughter filtered to them on the breeze. Mai glanced up the beach. Chip and Noah walked side by side. Noah had the football tucked under his arm.

Dale left her arm around Mai's shoulder for a moment before she stepped away. Her face was flushed red. "I'm going to get—I'll get the cooler. They'll be hungry when they get back."

She stepped back and stumbled. Mai took a step toward her and caught her arm, righting her. A flash of desire swept over Mai as her fingers closed around Dale's forearm.

"Thank you." Dale stared into Mai's eyes and Mai lost herself in her golden-brown gaze. She slipped her arm free of Mai's grip. Turned and quickstepped toward the parking lot.

The kite string jerked, and Mai tightened her hold on the winder, fighting a gust of wind and her own desires.

*

Dale unzipped her sweatshirt and stripped it off. The cold spring wind bit into the skin on her bare arms and she trudged on with her head down. Her body burned everywhere she had pressed against Mai's lithe body.

After reaching the safety of the truck, she fished the keys from her pocket and opened the rear door. The cooler with the lunch Mai had prepared sat on the floor behind the driver's seat. Her body ached with need. *How long has it been since I was drawn to someone like I'm drawn to Mai? Which is stupid. And wrong. And why does she have to look so damn sexy in her jeans and sweatshirt?*

Dale yanked the lid off the cooler. She dug around for a small piece of ice and rubbed it over her forehead and down her throat over her flushed skin. Her nipples peaked against the lace of her bra, responding to the chill. "Great, now I'm on high-beams." She tossed the small bit of ice aside and pressed her hands to her breasts in an attempt to warm them.

Stirred by her hug with Mai, the warmth of her palms had the opposite effect. She gasped as her nipples hardened even more. Want, low and hungry, stirred in her belly.

She closed her eyes, confident the massive truck door and her position blocked her from anyone's view, and gave her nipples a tweak. Her body responded and a gush of wet soaked her jeans. *Would they miss me if I climbed into the back of the crew cab and took care of myself?* It would take Mai at least an hour for her to wind in the kite and the boys were occupied. Dale bit her lip to stifle her groan of frustration as she rolled her nipples.

"Need help?"

Mai's voice behind her startled Dale and she yipped and yanked her hands away from her chest. "Um, what?" Heat rose in her face. *Did she see me? Oh no. She must think I'm a perv. Fuck. And she wants to help?*

"With the cooler? I packed it pretty heavy." Mai's voice was even.

"Oh well, um, sure." Dale wiped a hand over her brow, catching a stray drop of sweat before it rolled into her eye. "Who's minding your kite?"

"Noah and Chip."

Dale stepped away from the truck. Keeping her back toward Mai she pulled her sweatshirt on and zipped it up to her neck. "That'd be great." She leaned over the cooler and pulled a blanket from the backseat of the truck and draped it over the top of the cooler. Lifting up on the handle, she dragged the cooler to the edge of the door.

Mai reached back to grab the other handle. "Back in the day I'd have thrown this up on my shoulder and strutted down the beach with it to impress women."

Dale laughed. "What happened? You don't feel the need to impress me?"

"I blew out my shoulder playing volleyball. Now I impress women with my cooking."

Dale pushed aside the wave of jealousy nipping at her. *So what? So what if she cooked for other people? She's a chef. It's what she does. It's not like we're dating or anything. What would it look like if she were trying to impress me? Her everyday cooking is divine. Let it go. Not going there. I need to get some action. I'm thirsty that's all.*

They carried the cooler between them until they reached the spot where Noah and Chip were winding the kite in. They placed it on the sand. With a quick snap of her wrists Mai opened the blanket. Dale caught the edge as it flapped in the wind and they spread it out over the sand.

Mai drew a small bottle of hand sanitizer from her jacket pocket and used it. She tossed it to Dale. Dale caught it and squirted a dollop in her hands.

The kite fluttered to the sand. Noah trotted to it, unclipped the string, and rolled it up.

"Can I help, Ms. Miller?" Chip knelt on the blanket.

Dale passed the sanitizer to him. "Take one this to Noah. And use some yourself."

Mai placed a thick dishcloth on the blanket and arranged covered dishes of various sizes around a cutting board. In minutes, she had arranged three different cheeses, all perfectly sliced, on the board along with various types of crackers.

With a flourish Mai pointed at a cluster of three dishes. "Black olive tapenade, sun-dried tomato spread, and sweet pepper jelly." She uncovered a sectioned tray of sliced apples, toasted nuts, and dates and placed it next to the cheese board.

Noah and Chip sat on the edge of the blanket with their shoes off to the side. Mai held up a dark-green bottle with gold foil around the top. "Cider?"

"Non-alcoholic, right?" Dale inclined her head toward the boys.

"Of course." Mai passed four glasses out.

With practiced motions she opened the cider and poured them each a serving of the bubbling golden liquid. After wedging the bottle into the sand keep it upright, she lifted her glass. "To sunny days and good friends."

Dale lifted her glass and sipped her cider. *Friends. That's how she sees me. Friends. And that's all it can be. Damn it.*

Chip and Noah plowed through the food like they had not eaten in a week. Dale nibbled the offerings, her stomach in knots with the realization of her feelings for Mai. She studied her from under her lashes. Mai talked and joked with Chip and Noah about gaming and sports and things Dale could only imagine what the hell they were talking about.

When had it happened? When had she become so disconnected from her son? From everything that didn't have to do with her business. Molly had been happy for Dale to work. Her hobby had been spending money as fast as Dale made it. And Dale had been too willing to work. A slave to Molly's charms, she had worked so much she had lost touch with her kids.

"What or who is a LARP?" Dale rolled the plastic tumbler between her hands.

"Live action role-play, Mom. And it's role-playing games where you dress up and act like your character. There's different themes and games and stuff."

Dale turned to Mai. "Do you do that?"

Mai grinned. "I haven't but it sounds like fun. I loved tabletop role-playing games as a kid."

Dale shook her head. "I missed so much getting married when I did."

Noah frowned. "Do you regret it, Mom?"

Dale cupped his face. "Not for a minute."

Noah blushed and leaned back from Dale's touch. Chip looked away for the tender moment.

Dale crossed her legs and leaned back on her hands. "Chip, do you do LARPing?"

Chip looked down at his hands. "No. But my mom is big into it."

"No kidding?" Mai sat forward. "Where does your mom play?"

Dale sipped from her glass, stung by Mai's interest in Chip's mom, Sally.

"She has a group in Cleveland she plays with." Chip hid his face in his hands. "It's so embarrassing."

Mai laughed. "But why? She's having fun. What's the problem?" She took a bite of an apple and chewed slowly.

"Last time it was a fairy tale theme and she left our house dressed as Red Riding Hood in fishnet stockings, thigh high boots, and a red corset." Chip rolled his eyes.

Dale squeezed Chip's shoulder. "You do know we parents sit up at night trying to think of ways to embarrass our kids, right?"

Mai picked up the bottle of cider and waggled it. "Who wants refills?" She topped up Noah's glass and then emptied the rest into Dale's cup. She raised an eyebrow. "Who would you go as if you were to role-play?"

Dale smoothed her hand over her jeans. "Not much for fairy tales. And I haven't put a costume on in years."

Mai trailed a finger over Dale's forearm. "Have you read *The Lord of the Rings*? You'd make a great Galadriel. 'Instead of a Dark Lord, you would have a queen, not dark but beautiful and terrible as the dawn. Tempestuous as the sea, and stronger than the foundations of the earth. All shall love me and despair.'"

Dale stilled, captured by Mai's dark gaze as she spoke. Her eyes held mischief and an invitation.

Noah coughed loudly and Dale snapped her gaze to him. "Mom, is it okay if I ride back with Chip?"

"Sure." Dale busied herself with clearing up their picnic, desperate to ignore the blaze of desire burning through her soul.

Chapter Seven

Mai stirred the pan of simmering tomatoes, onions, and black olives as she added fresh thyme. The scent of the herb bloomed as it heated. "The key to herbs is heating them enough to release their flavor but not cooking them to oblivion."

Noah stood to her left and peered over her shoulder. "How do you know how much heat is too much?"

"Practice. Cooking is about experience and sensory memory. And a willingness to experiment. A good cook keeps track of experiments. Next time you can tweak it, or leave it as is if you were happy with the results."

Noah jotted notes in a spiral notebook as Mai spoke. "Got it."

"Fresh herbs are delicate, and you need to use different amounts from dried herbs."

The scent of lemon verbena overrode the fragrance of the sauce. The unmistakable sound of pumps tap-tapping across the floor made Mai look up from the pan. She turned toward the dining area.

Dale stood at the table sorting through a black clutch. Mai raked her gaze over her, starting at the black strapped pumps on her feet, up over the tanned bare legs, to the hem of the bright-red knee-length shirtwaist short-sleeve dress. Nipped at the waist, with three buttons undone the dress showed off Dale's stunning cleavage and broad shoulders.

"Wow," Mai murmured.

"You look great!" Noah's enthusiastic comment echoed in Mai's ears.

Dale strode into the kitchen, lifted her chin, and inhaled. "That smells divine."

Mai's gaze drifted over Dale's long graceful neck. Her hair was combed back, and soft honey-brown waves fell about her shoulders. A vision of herself threading her fingers through Dale's hair, tugging it to arch her neck back and then kissing her way along the smooth skin of her throat until she ended up at the delicate hollow between her collarbones, filled Mai's mind.

The sharp scent of tomatoes on the edge of burning startled her from her daydream. She forced herself to shift her gaze back to the stove. She turned the burner off and moved the pan off the heat.

Dale sauntered to the door and the fabric of her dress swayed around her ample hips. "Makes me sorry I'm not going to be here for dinner."

"Me too." At Dale's raised eyebrow Mai continued, "I mean, Noah wanted you to try his pasta."

"Made from scratch." Noah grinned at his mother.

"Did you finish your homework?"

"Yeah. Mai helped me."

A brief frown crossed Dale's face before she smoothed her features. "Don't take advantage of Mai, Noah. She's not here to tutor you."

"I didn't do anything. He did the work himself." Mai jumped to Noah's defense. "And I don't mind. I wouldn't do it if I did."

"It's not part of our agreement. I don't want you to feel pressured." She pulled her phone from her purse and glanced at the screen. "I have to run. Don't wait up."

"'Kay." Noah tilted his head at his mother. "Where ya going?"

"Free concert at the college. Ms. Rice asked me to go." Dale left in a swirl of red silk.

The scent of her perfume faded. Mai blinked. Her shoulders tightened. *A date? Wait. Why should I care? Because I do. Damn that dress. Let it go. Not your business.*

Mai moved back to the stove. She chewed her lip as she stirred the cooling sauce to break up the tomatoes into bite-size pieces. She stabbed at a particularly stubborn tomato and a bit of sauce slopped over, sizzling as it ran down the side of the pan. *Focus. This a business arrangement. Nothing more.*

"How much water for the pasta? Is it different because it's fresh?" Noah's voice drew her from her thoughts.

Mai forced a smile and placed the spoon on a small plate before she turned him. "It is. We need a large pot. The most important part is you need at least three times as much water as the amount of pasta you're cooking. And the water must be as salty as broth. Pasta is made without salt. If you don't salt the water, it tastes like paste."

Noah dragged a large pot out from the lower cabinet and lowered it into the sink. Water splashed against the metal of the pot.

Mai fiddled with the hem of her shirt. "So, who is Ms. Rice?"

"One of my granddad's friends. Her husband died last year. Mom fixes stuff for her all the time for free."

Mai exhaled sharply. *Not a date.* "Good. That's good. Nice of your mom to do that."

Noah cocked his head at Mai, and a sly smile crossed his face. "You like my mom, don't you?"

Mai avoided his gaze. "What's not to like? She's kind and capable." *And smart and hot as hell and just my type and oh man is this trouble.*

Noah straightened and shut the tap off. "I know you like *like* her. I followed your show. I know you're lesbian. So's Mom. It's cool."

Mai lifted the box of coarse salt off the counter and stared at Noah. "You followed my show? How old were you? Like when you were ten?"

Noah blushed. "Yeah, Charlene was hot."

Mai shrugged. "Well, just because your mom and I are into women doesn't mean I'm interested in your mom."

Noah peered into her eyes, his gaze intense. "You suck at lying." He turned away and lifted the pot from the sink and placed it on the stove. With a firm spin of the dial he turned the burner on full. Blue and yellow flames shot up the sides of the pot.

Mai snorted. "I know."

Chapter Eight

Dale leaned over the plans she had drawn up for the building renovation. The fruity scent of olive oil heating in a pan wafted from the kitchen. She glanced toward Mai and Noah as they bent over the stove, shoulders touching.

"Ease the garlic into the pan and then watch it closely. We want to brown it, not obliterate it." Mai's voice as she schooled Noah settled over Dale. And she watched fascinated as her youngest child paid rapt attention to Mai.

"There. Get them out now. If you let them go another second, the garlic will taste burnt."

Noah scooped the cloves from the pan and on to a plate.

"Fantastic. Now. Turn the flame off and move the pan. The surface is still hot. You don't want to overheat the oil."

Noah moved quickly to follow Mai's direction.

Dale's mouth watered. "What are you making?"

Noah turned and grinned at his mother. "Garlic infused oil to go over the pasta we're going to make when I get home from practice."

Dale heart squeezed with her son's enthusiasm. Mai's quiet encouragement and affection for her son was palpable. What would it be like to have a partner who liked her kids? Molly never had. Dale's kids had been the source of endless arguments.

Dale clenched her jaw as the memory of Molly slapping Noah's face surfaced. That had been the beginning of the end. Dale still couldn't believe she had been so seduced by Molly's attention she let her almost destroy her relationship with Noah.

She pushed aside her guilt over not being able to pay for cooking school because she'd believed Molly's lies. After Molly left, taking all of Dale's savings and most of the money in her business accounts, Dale had worked sixteen-hour days to keep their house and put food on the table.

Noah had stepped up and managed most of the household tasks since then. Four years after near bankruptcy she was able to help Thomas with his tuition. But culinary school was still out of reach for Noah, and after watching his older friends struggle with crippling student debt, he wouldn't even apply for the slickly packaged loans offered by the bank.

"Mom?" Noah's hand on her shoulder startled her.

"Sorry, what?"

"I'm leaving now. I've got practice."

"Oh. Be safe." Dale patted his hand.

"Always." Noah trotted out of the kitchen with his sports bag over his shoulder.

"He's a good kid." Mai swished water into the cup she was washing.

"He is." Dale tapped the drawings. "Do you want to look at these? These are what I'm going to submit for the building engineer."

"Sure." Mai dried her hands on the dish towel. "You want some water?" She dropped ice cubes into a tall glass as she spoke.

"No. Thank you."

After filling her glass, she rounded the bar separating the dining room from the kitchen. The nearness of Mai's body as she leaned over Dale's shoulder and studied the drawings ruined Dale's concentration.

"This here. Is this how the living area will be laid out?"

Dale traced her finger over the printouts. "It's hard to see on this but it's open plan as we discussed with all the accessibility features and requirements in place." Dale turned her head to look up at Mai. "Do you want an elevator installed instead of the stair lift? I can do it. We'd lose a bit of the dining area but not too much."

"Will it add much? It would be good for Yvonne."

"Not too much. But I need include it on the permit and plans." Dale pulled her tablet closer and tapped in some notes. "Does Yvonne have mobility issues?"

Mai straightened. "Yes. She's good with a walker or cane most days. But it could get worse at any time." Her eyes shuttered. "The plans look good, as far as I can tell. Thank you." She walked back to the kitchen and busied herself with washing a plate. She dragged open the dishwasher and placed it inside to dry. "How come your dishwasher doesn't work?"

Dale flushed. "I haven't had time to fix it."

Mai raised her eyebrow. "Noah said it's been three years."

"It has." Dale fidgeted with her pen.

"Why?"

"Why what? It wasn't a priority."

"Because Noah does the dishes? He won't be here forever. You'll need it when he leaves home."

Dale shoved away from the table. "I'll try to get it fixed." Shame welled up. Why hadn't she fixed it? Because she had been broke when it stopped working and then, when she had a little breathing room, there had been Thomas's tuition to pay. Some bill was always more important than replacing the dishwasher. She turned away from Mai's accusing stare.

"Is it something I could help with?"

Dale gathered her forms and plans together in a loose pile. "I doubt it. I think the whole thing is shot. It's at least twenty-five years old. I don't have money to buy a new one, or the time to install it." She waved the sheaf of paper at Mai. "Your renovation is not the only project I have right now."

Mai flinched. "Got it. Sorry I asked." She turned her back on Dale and went back to washing the dishes.

"Mai?"

Mai turned toward Dale, her lips pressed into a thin line, and she knotted the dish towel in her hands.

"I didn't mean to be sharp. I apologize. I know it looks like I take Noah for granted but I don't. I'm doing the best I can with what I have."

Mai tilted her head to the side and her gaze skittered away from Dale. "I think you're a great mom. I didn't mean to speak out of turn."

The earnest tone of her voice had Dale biting her lip to stop the prick of tears threatening her control. "Thank you. I don't deserve accolades but thank you."

"It must have been hard. Being alone, raising them alone." Mai hung the dishcloth to dry.

"It was. My dad and mom helped as much as they could. They were both still working full time then. Dad was making guitars on the side, trying to build his own business."

A chime sounded. Mai tugged her phone from her pocket and glanced at the screen. "Gotta take this." Mai walked to the basement door and thumbed her phone on. "Hey! Yeah, I got your email." Her voice faded as she walked down the steps.

Dale brooded as she carried her coffee cup to the kitchen and placed it on the counter. *Who is she so happy to talk to? Not me.* She grimaced when she remembered the way Mai had flinched during their conversation. Bright-blue numbers on the stove displayed the time, taunting Dale. *Noon. I could at least check it out.* Dale emptied the plates from the dishwasher and dried them before she put them away.

She turned the water off under the sink. Using her phone as a flashlight she studied the plumbing tie-in. She eyed the frayed electric wiring leading to the dishwasher. A chill ran through her. She closed her eyes against the images of Noah receiving a lethal shock because of her negligence and trembled.

The sound of Mai's voice filtered through the basement as Dale made her way to the circuit breaker box. She pulled the lever and shut the power down to the entire house, not willing to risk a shock or trust the past homeowner's barely legible notes beside the breaker bars.

She took the basement stairs two at a time and made a quick trip to the garage for the toolbox she kept for home repairs. Kneeling on the floor, she removed everything from the cabinet and set to work to make things right.

Chapter Nine

Dale woke to the warm smell of bread baking. She scrabbled for her phone and checked the time. *Six. Who the fuck is baking at six on a Saturday morning?* She shifted the pillow over her head. Her stomach growled, an audible reminder she had skipped dinner to make the concert the night before. *Mai. That's who.*

Her impetuous decision to barter a place to stay with Mai in exchange for Noah's cooking lessons bubbled up. *What was I thinking? And why did she take me up on my offer? Is she telling the truth? Or is she broke and playing me?* Dale rolled to her back, rested her hands on her chest, and stared at the ceiling. After Molly had left, Dale had been so hurt she hadn't dated at all for the first year. Since then it had been a string of disastrous dates she'd arranged via a dating app she had signed up for in a fit of self-pity.

Doesn't seem like the type to lie. But neither did Molly. She's not Molly. So damn calm. Intense. And sexy as fuck. She closed her eyes and a vision of Mai dressed in fitted jeans and sparkling white T-shirt tight enough to show off her toned arms filled Dale's mind before giving over to a vision of her eyes and teasing smile.

Dale's eyes fluttered closed as she remembered her view of Mai changing in her car. *How would it be to have her under me and scatter kisses over her exquisite back? To kiss her. Slide my hands over those thighs?* She stifled a groan and cupped her breasts. She squeezed and pinched her nipples, imagining Mai's mouth on them.

A rill of pleasure shot through her body along with a sharp wave of desire. She slipped her hand down her sleep pants and into her wet curls. She lifted her hips, arching into her palm. Dale drew her fingers along her slick folds. With the pad of her finger she rubbed the tip of her clit slowly, the touch exquisite and intense.

She brought herself close to coming before she thrust two fingers inside and stroked them in and out. A harsh bolt of pleasure crashed through her and she came without a sound, curled around her hand. She lay there until her breathing slowed. *Pathetic. Rubbing one out fantasizing about a client. What is wrong with me*? She kicked the covers off and scrambled out of the bed, stripped off her T-shirt and pajama pants, and tossed them in the direction of the hamper. In the bathroom, she turned the shower on full, avoiding the mirror, unwilling to witness the desperation she was sure showed on her face.

*

Mai pulled her favorite knife out of her knife roll. She hefted it, the familiar weight comforting in her palm. The kitchen was her safe space. Her world. A sense of peace settled over her as she set about her prep work. She placed the onion on the cutting board, sliced it in half, and peeled the outer skin off. Working quickly, she repeated the actions until she had the three pounds of onions peeled.

The entire house slept but for Mai and the old tabby cat perched on the printer in the dining room. She eyed Mai, her disdain for her disturbing her household evident. She sounded a sharp meow in Mai's direction before jumping from the printer to the table and then to the floor. Once on the floor she shot her another glare before stalking from the room.

The timer on Mai's phone sounded and she turned it off quickly. She opened the door and drew out the loaf pan. The smell of the fresh bread made her mouth water. She tilted the pan and the bread slid out and onto the cooling rack. A sound behind her made her turn. Dale stood with her hands on her hips. Her wet hair hung in tangles and the scent of citrus filled Mai's senses.

"Good morning." Mai placed the hot pan on top of the stove. "I hope I didn't wake you."

Dale frowned. "No. Well. Yes, but waking up to the smell of fresh bread is not all bad."

Mai turned to the sink. "Sorry. I'm always up early. I'll put some water on for your coffee."

"You don't have to... I mean, thank you." Dale's gaze slid along the counter. "Two scoops is just right." She turned her back to Mai.

"I brought in the paper." Mai filled the electric kettle and turned it on before she set up the French press, carefully measuring two scoops of coffee into the carafe.

"Thanks." Dale sat at the kitchen table, drew the stack of newspaper to her, and started reading.

Mai chewed her lip remembering her first encounter with pre-coffee Dale. Unwilling to deal with her before she had her morning fix, Mai picked up her knife and an onion half. With precise movements she made thin cuts along the onion's grain, the motions as natural to her as breathing.

Her attention drifted back to Dale. The early morning light filtering through the gauzy dining room window curtains highlighted her features. Mai was mesmerized by

Dale's high cheekbones, delicate nose, and bow-shaped mouth. Mai imagined crossing the kitchen and rubbing her thumb over Dale's plump lower lip before she bent down to kiss her. The sharp sting of the knife blade broke her trance, and blood bloomed across the cutting board. "Damn."

At that moment, the kettle sounded. Mai snatched a dish towel up and wrapped it around her finger.

Dale looked up and the scowl on her face morphed into wide-eyed fear. "What the fuck did you do to yourself?" She bolted from the table, reached around Mai, and unplugged the kettle. "For fuck's sake. Let me see."

Blood soaked through and stained the thin dishcloth and wet Mai's hand.

"I can't show you. I need to keep some pressure on it."

Dale raised her eyes to Mai's face and a visible shudder shook her frame. Face white, she rested her trembling fingers on Mai's shoulder.

"Are you okay?" Mai ignored the throb in her finger and looked at Dale's pale face.

"I'm not good with blood." Dale shifted on her feet.

"Go sit. I'm okay."

Dale shielded her eyes with her hand. "Yes. All right." She sat down and rested her forehead on the kitchen table.

Mai opened the towel and peeped at her finger. Blood surged up along the deep cut and a bit of white showed around the edges. "Um. Are you okay enough to drive me to the hospital?" She rewrapped the towel around her finger.

Dale raised her head from the table. "No. I'll wake Noah." She rasped as she lurched from the kitchen.

"Noah!" Her footsteps thundered on the wooden stairs as she climbed them two at a time. "Noah!" she shouted again as she charged up the stairs.

Mai sat down and waited for Noah and Dale to return. *This is going to need stitches. Cut myself because I couldn't stop looking at her. I'm an idiot.*

*

The early morning crowd at the emergency room was sparse. Mai stared at the pen and sign-in sheet, unwilling to let up the pressure she held on her cut. Dale signed her in and picked up the information clipboard.

Noah sat next to Mai, his brow wrinkled. "You should've woke me up. I wanted to go to the market."

Mai closed her eyes and sighed loudly.

Noah huffed. "I mean aren't you supposed to teach me how to buy vegetables and stuff? And if I'd been slicing the onions you wouldn't have cut yourself."

Dale opened her mouth to tell Noah to stow his attitude when Mai spoke up, exhaustion etched in her features.

"Set your alarm next time. Real cooks show up, Noah."

Dale glanced up, surprised at Mai's sharp tone, not that she would have been any less harsh. "Noah, give Mai a break."

Chastised, Noah turned his beet-red face toward the television mounted on the wall above the waiting room chairs. He folded his arms over his chest and slouched in his chair.

Dale nudged Mai's shoulder gently. "I need your ID and insurance card."

Mai leaned to her left. "Wallet's in my front pocket."

Dale looked away and dug her fingers into Mai's jeans, fighting hard and failing to ignore the intimacy of the moment and the heat of Mai's skin under the thin material of her pocket. She held the wallet out to Mai.

Mai arched an eyebrow. "Go ahead, it's not like I can." She cradled her hand close to her chest. "My ID is on the left. I don't have an insurance card."

"You don't have insurance?" Dale chewed her lip.

"Not at the moment." Mai lowered her chin to her chest.

"Does it hurt a lot?" Dale inclined her head at the bloody towel.

"Not bad. I've had worse. At least I didn't cut my fingertip off."

Dale swallowed the bile that rose in her throat at the image Mai's words conjured in her mind. "I'll put our address down for your local address."

"Thanks."

Mai leaned her head back against the wall. Her normally light-brown skin was pale and a bead of sweat shone on her upper lip. She stretched her legs out and crossed them at the ankle. Her hair hung in sweaty tendrils over her brow.

Dale reached up and brushed her fingertips over Mai's brow and pushed the hair off her forehead before she moved her hand down and cupped her face.

Mai started and opened her eyes. Her gaze settled on Dale's face. "Feels nice."

Dale inhaled sharply at the longing she saw in Mai's eyes. She yanked her hand back and bolted from her chair. She clutched the clipboard with both hands and hugged it to her chest. "I'll give this to the nurse."

She turned away from Mai. *Great. What a wonderful way to send the wrong message. But is it wrong? She seemed okay with it. But am I?* Guilt settled over Dale and she forced herself to not look back, afraid of what Mai would see in her eyes.

*

Mai's hand throbbed. Fifteen stitches. Another bill that would chip away at her cash. She groaned and flipped her pillow over and pressed her face to the cool cotton. The adrenaline rush that had accompanied her injury faded, leaving her chilled and sick to her stomach.

A tap at the door echoed in the room. "Yeah?"

"May I come in? I brought you some tea and crackers." Dale's voice and the memory of her hand on Mai's face made Mai's heart race.

"Yes. Of course." Mai pushed herself up to sitting and winced when her hand bumped against the bed.

Dale swept in the room, a cup of tea in one hand and a plate of saltine crackers in the other. "I thought you might need a little something." She placed the plate on the nightstand.

Mai rolled the edge of her T-shirt in her hand. "Thanks." She took a cracker and nibbled at it.

Dale's posture was ramrod straight. "I need to apologize to you." Her gaze was fixed on her clasped hands in her lap.

Mai frowned. "For what?"

"For touching you the way I did in the waiting room. I don't—" Dale broke off, stood, and then began to pace in the small room. "I don't want you to get the wrong idea."

"About what?" May set aside her cracker.

"About me. Us. I mean I don't want you to think I'm going to take liberties or expect anything. We have a business arrangement. I want to keep it that way."

A cold wave of sadness settled over Mai. "I get it. I didn't think anything of it." *Liar.* "Other than I was in pain and you were doing what a friend might do."

Dale stopped pacing and placed her hands on her hips. "That's good." She waved her toward the tea and crackers. "I'll come back and check on you later, unless you want me to leave you alone."

"I'm fine." Mai lifted the teacup to her mouth and took a sip. "And thank you, I appreciate your honesty."

Dale lifted her chin. "I've got to go out for a bit. Call Noah if you need anything. And you're welcome. I always think it's best to be clear."

The sharp taste of the tea matched the stab of disappointment that twisted her gut as Dale left the room.

*

Her basement room was cozy in an animal den sort of way. The dank smell of the cement walls had dissipated after the window was opened. The sound of crickets chirping echoed in the dark space. *What was that touching thing in the waiting room?* Mai's body tightened and a ripple of heat spread from her chest to her clit. *She acted like she cared. And her eyes. Hungry. Fuck no. I can't do this. She said no mixing business and pleasure. I need to focus. Get the restaurant done so I can bring Yvonne here so we can be together again. Family. Or what's left of it. I need some action. I'm desperate for touch, that's all.*

Mai rolled to her side and swiped her phone off the nightstand. She winced when the bright light of the screen hit her eyes as she thumbed it on. Three screens later she tapped to open the dating app Hit Me Up.

Strictly for women looking to meet other women who were into kink, she still couldn't believe she'd let Yvonne talk her into signing up for it. Despondent after breaking up with Charlene, Mai had been so dismally disappointed after her first date from a random right swipe she hadn't used the app again.

After logging in, she changed her location settings and updated her interest level from "long-term" to "casual." Mai changed her screen name to Chillone and altered a few bits in her bio. With that finished, she scrolled through the profiles matching her parameters and bobbled her phone when Dale's photo crossed her screen.

Mai gazed at the photo Dale had used for her profile under the screen name of HamerNnails. A sleeveless white shirt showed off Dale's tanned muscular arms and a single strand of pearls circled her graceful neck. The collar of the shirt was open and displayed her deep cleavage. Her posture was relaxed at a table, and she looked over the top of a pair of classic Ray-Ban sunglasses as she stared into the camera. Mai's hand trembled as she remembered how being the focus of Dale's gaze in the waiting room had made her feel. How much she wanted to have Dale over her, looking at Mai like she was the center of the universe.

Mai scrolled past the photo. *She's down for casual sex. How that would be? Nope. Never going to mix business with pleasure again. But I'd like to.*

A notification message flashed across her phone screen and Mai opened the message.

Ur hot AF. Want to meet?

From user Bedtornado.

That's your opening line? Srsly? Maybe.

Mai pressed send. She rested the back of her hand on her forehead. Her phone vibrated in her palm and she flicked open the response to her message.

Yeah. Why waste time? You down for it or not? Wanna meet for dinner first? We can pretend it's a date.

Mai chuckled to herself and checked out Bedtornado's profile picture. It was from the top of her legs down, and her long legs were showcased by thigh high stockings and black pumps. A pair of handcuffs dangled from a well-manicured hand.

Yeah. I'm down. Or will be. Dinner first sounds good. Mai sent her reply and scrolled back to Dale's profile and traced her finger over Dale's photo. *Not for me. Not this time.*

Chapter Ten

The overhead light flared on and Mai bolted upright. A tall shaggy-haired man stood in the doorway. Mai grabbed her book off the nightstand and flung it at the intruder as she scrambled from the bed. "Get the fuck out of here!"

The man screamed when the book hit him in the face.

A flood of adrenaline ripped through her as she grabbed her phone. A sharp stab of pain made her eyes water when she banged her bandaged finger on the table. Swallowing the bile in her throat, she jabbed the emergency button to dial 9-1-1.

"The fuck you doin' in my room?" The stranger took a step closer.

Mai set her feet, fist cocked, ready to fight. She bit her lip against the pain in her bandaged hand.

"What?" Mai gripped her phone tightly, her palms sweaty.

The dispatcher's voice came over the line. "Nine-one-one, what is your emergency?"

"Fuck. Seth, the hell are you doing here in the middle of the night?" Dale's voice was rough with sleep and a short length of black pipe dangled from her hand. "Mai, hang up, it's my son."

"What?"

"Nine-one-one, what is your emergency?" The operator's voice was louder this time.

"Hang up." Dale grabbed her son's arm and yanked him toward her. "The fuck you doing, Seth? You're lucky I didn't hit you with a pipe."

Mai raised the phone to her ear. "Sorry. Misunderstanding, operator." The loud click of the dispatcher as she hung up stung Mai's ear. She flushed as she realized she was dressed only in boxers and a thin tank top. She crossed her arms over her chest.

Seth turned toward Dale. "I walked in on Eileen fucking Paul." His face twisted in pain. "And then she kicked me out." His voice was soft, and Mai had to strain to hear his words.

After placing the pipe on the dresser, Dale wrapped her arms around her son and hugged him close. A good six inches taller than her, he leaned down and buried his head against Dale's neck. The tight sounds of his muffled sobs tugged at Mai's heart.

Dale hugged Seth and murmured soothing sounds as she rubbed his back. Mai took advantage of their distraction and pulled on her jeans. Uncomfortable with the intimacy of the moment, Mai picked up her paperback book and placed it back on the nightstand.

Seth straightened and gestured to Mai. "Um, should I look for another place?" His eyes were bloodshot, and he swiped at his nose with his sleeve.

"No." Mai stuffed her phone in her pocket. "I'll go. I can find a place for tonight and look for another place tomorrow. Family belongs together." Mai shoved aside the burn of other memories of leaving in the night with only her clothes as she bent and gathered her clothes and stuffed them into her duffel.

"Stop. Mai, it's two in the morning for fuck's sake. Seth, go sleep on the couch. We'll sort this tomorrow."

Dale pushed her hair back with both hands. The unguarded expression and worry on her face for her son made Mai's breath hitch.

Seth lifted his shoulders and sniffed. "M'kay, Mom." He squinted at Mai. "Sorry, I scared you." He rubbed at the red mark on his cheek where the book had struck him. "But who are you and why are you sleeping in my room?"

"Mai. I'm Mai. Your mom's..."

"Seth, I said we'd talk in the morning. Go to bed." Dale's sharp words cut their conversation off.

Seth nodded and sighed in acknowledgment of Dale's words. He pushed past her with his head bowed. His heavy tread on the stairs echoed over their heads as he made his way to the kitchen. Mai turned her attention to Dale.

She was barefoot and wrapped in a light-blue satin dressing gown that ended at her thighs. The blood-red polish on her toes and the delicate arch of her foot drew Mai's gaze. Unwanted visions of herself tracing the lines of Dale's beautifully manicured feet with her tongue before kissing her way up her thighs filled Mai's head as she stared.

The hair on the back of Mai's neck stood up as she sensed Dale's eyes on her. She straightened and met Dale's gaze. Dale stepped closer, lifted her chin, and raised an eyebrow. The knowing look on her face made Mai flush and she dropped her gaze. The moment stretched out between them. Dale lifted her hand as if to reach for Mai's shoulder before she lowered her hand and stepped back.

"I told him she was bad news. It's been going on for a while. He didn't believe me when I told him I'd seen Paul's truck outside his house when he was at work."

Mai tilted her head and studied Dale's face from under her lashes. "We all make those kinds of mistakes. And when you're in love you're willing to believe anything, even when your eyes and gut tell you different."

Dale snorted. "True that." She yawned. "Sorry about the drama." At the doorway she paused and looked over her shoulder. "Nice tank top by the way."

A slow smile curled her mouth and Mai shivered. Dale turned and walked away. Mai sat down hard on the bed and dropped her head in her hands, fully aware of the faint scent of Dale's sleep-warm body hanging in the air and the tension between them.

*

Dale sat at the kitchen bar and sipped her coffee. A black nitrile glove covered Mai's bandaged hand as she stirred a bowl of eggs, her hand a blur as she whisked the whites and yolks together. The rhythmic scrape of the metal whisk paused as she added a dollop of cream. The sound of the delicate scrape of the whisk resumed.

Dale marveled at how quickly she had become accustomed to the exquisite omelets Mai whipped up for her every Sunday morning. The harsh notes of Seth's snores from the couch brought Dale back to the problem at hand.

"Once you've got the roof done, I could go back to the apartment."

"No. That's not the deal we made, and even with a roof the place is not fit to live in." Dale grit her teeth as she thought about the risk Mai had taken sleeping in the apartment. "We're not doing that. And Noah likes having you here."

Mai chewed her lip and placed the sauté pan on the stovetop before she lit the flame. "Noah's a great kid." She poured the creamy yellow egg mixture into the pan and scattered fresh marjoram over the top.

"I know you want to put everything toward the renovation. Renting a room somewhere would cut into your money." Dale took a deep breath and traced the woodgrain pattern of the bar, avoiding Mai's eyes. "Would you mind sharing my room?"

She glanced up and into Mai's startled face and swallowed on a dry throat as she realized what she had said.

"I mean you could keep your clothes there. I didn't mean...I mean if you wouldn't mind sleeping on the couch." A loud snore from Seth punctuated the quiet morning. Dale inclined her head toward the living room. "He snores like a bear. I hear him in my room. Thomas slept right through it when they shared a room, but even with their door closed it kept Noah and me up. It's why we moved him to the basement."

Mai took a plate from the counter. "I could do that." She turned the perfectly browned omelet on the plate and placed it in front of Dale. "You sure you don't mind?"

Dale flushed under Mai's direct gaze. "No. I mean...it's your clothes. What's the big deal?"

"Ugh, my ears. Mom, why is Seth on the couch?" Noah padded into the kitchen. His hair stuck up around his ears and he rubbed his eyes.

Dale scowled. "Eileen."

"I wondered when that was going to blow up. Good riddance."

Dale cut a bite of omelet and scooped it up with her fork. The subtle flavor of herbs and eggs was divine. She barely stifled her moan as she wiped her mouth. "Mai, you could make a killing selling these omelets."

Noah slid off his stool. "We ought to set up at the farmer's market. The crepe lady went on vacation, and no one else has anything but bread and buns."

He opened the refrigerator, took a package of spinach out, and placed it on the counter. After sorting through the shelves, he placed a wedge of Swiss cheese next to the greens. He took the grater from its place on the shelf, grated the cheese into a small bowl, and passed it to Mai.

Mai turned to Noah. "How do you get a spot? And I'd need something to cook on."

"You ask the organizer." As he spoke Noah filled a bowl with cold water and then he dunked the spinach up and down to wash it. Using a sheet of paper towel from the roll, he dried the greens carefully before he tore the leaves into bite-size pieces. "Lots of time folks pay for a spot and then bail halfway through the season. And Grandpa has a two-burner camp stove. I bet he'd let you borrow it."

Mai sat next to Dale at the counter. She pulled over Noah's spiral notebook, turned to a blank page at the back, and began scribbling notes, her brow furrowed. "It might work." She looked up at Noah. "You going to make my omelet?"

Noah moved to the stove and Dale marveled at her son's confident movements as he made Mai a Swiss cheese and spinach omelet. He placed the creation in front of her.

Dale sipped her coffee and turned to watch Mai.

She lifted the edge of the omelet and inspected the bottom of it before she turned her fork on edge and cut a bite. She lifted the steaming morsel to her mouth and closed her lips over it. She chewed slowly.

Dale studied the anxious expression on Noah's face as he filled his juice glass and observed Mai.

"Take it off the heat and plate it ten seconds sooner. The eggs will finish cooking on the plate, and it will be more tender. And you did an excellent job balancing the amount of cheese and spinach. It's not too wet and you can taste both flavors. Too many folks ruin omelets by adding too much cheese." She lifted her hand and Noah fist-bumped her, a broad grin on his face.

"Geez, what is this, *America's Next Great Chef?*" Seth crossed the kitchen and hip checked Noah out of the way, yanked a cabinet open, and snagged a coffee cup with one finger. "What'cha going to make me for breakfast, Tiny Tot?"

Noah shoved back. Seth rocked back on his heels and barely managed to set his cup on the counter before Noah wrapped his arms around Seth's waist and lifted him off his feet. Seth jabbed his fingers into Noah's side. Noah shrieked with laughter, let go, and crumpled to the floor as Seth tickled him relentlessly. The brothers scuffled, laughing and taunting each other. The loud bang of Noah's foot striking a cabinet rang out.

"First one breaks something fixes it," Dale shouted over their laughter.

The boys rose from the floor and straightened up. Seth touched two fingers to his brow. "Aye, aye, Mom."

"Troublemaker." Dale laughed, crumpled her napkin, and tossed it at Seth. "And there better be enough coffee for me to have another cup."

"On it, Mom." Seth grinned and snatched up Dale's cup to refill it. He placed it gently on the counter in front of her.

Mai touched Dale's arm, drawing her attention. "I'd like to stay. I'm cool with the couch." She gestured to the column of figures in front of her. "I think Noah's on to something. Do you think your dad would lend me his cooktop? It'd mean I'd be out of here sooner."

Dale's heart squeezed tight at Mai's words and she pushed her reluctance aside, ignoring the wave of despair that washed over her at the thought of Mai leaving. Of course, she would leave. She was only here because it was a way back to her own place. This was a pit stop on her way to a new life. And settling down with Yvonne. Dale shrugged. "Let me finish my coffee and we'll go ask him."

Mai straightened. "Sure. I'd like to meet your folks."

"My dad. My mom passed when Noah was in kindergarten."

"Sorry." Mai's fingertips rested on Dale's forearm.

Dale stared at her hand and the simple gesture and kind tone of Mai's voice widened the space in her heart Mai had come to occupy.

Chapter Eleven

Wildflowers, a riot of yellow, red, and white, lined the long drive leading to Dale's father's house. Farmland stood to both sides of the highway, herds of cows dotted the scrubby fields, and fields of corn were broken up by plots of soybeans. They passed a field filled with pumpkin vines.

"Graber's still do pick-your-own pumpkins?" Mai rubbed the edge of her bandage where the skin itched.

"Yeah. They've expanded it. Hayrides, games for the kids, a big slide. Food trucks on Saturday." Dale flicked the turn signal on.

She turned onto a dirt road and slowed to a crawl as dust flared along the side of the truck. A two-story house painted barn red with dark-blue shutters and a wrap-around porch surrounded by tidy beds of roses sat at the end of the lane. An oak tree taller than the house with a tire swing suspended by a ratty gray rope shaded the front lawn. Mai rolled the edge of her T-shirt between her fingers and chewed her lip.

Dale parked behind a black jeep with an "if you can read this, I'm upside down" sticker on the back. "My dad's a bit much, no filter, but he's been the best."

Mai huffed out a breath. *Why am I worried about her dad? Hell, it's not like we're dating.* "My grandpa had zero chill. I'm good." She opened her door and stepped out of the truck.

Dale led them around the house to a white-painted workshop with three bays. "This was the old carriage house. My dad converted it into a workshop when he moved here after my mom died."

The first bay was open and the sounds of Pavarotti singing "Nessun dorma" played. They entered the cool interior. A tall man rose from the stool he had been sitting on. His hair was a cloud of white above a ruddy face and his beard was plaited in three tight braids secured with black bands. Tinted glasses hid his eyes, and a faded pale green T-shirt with "Age of Asparagus" emblazoned on the front hung off his gaunt frame. A broad grin split his face. "Dale!" He set aside a small hand plane.

"Who's your friend?" He stuck his hand out. "Eli Miller."

"Mai Li. Nice to meet you."

His grip was warm, and he pumped her arm twice before he dropped it. "Let me turn my music down."

Mai spun in a slow circle and marveled at the display of tools and guitars in various stages of completion. "This is amazing. I've never seen a guitar workshop."

Dale waved toward another part of the workshop. "Guitars and mandolins. He has a partner who works the renaissance fairs to sell them."

Eli returned and draped his arm over Dale's shoulder. "To what do I owe the pleasure of your company this morning?" He turned to Mai and looked her over. "You're not her usual type. Too much sincerity rolling off you."

Dale moved from under her father's arm. "Dad. For fuck's sake. We aren't dating." She walked over to the stool and sat down and glared at her father. "Are you high?"

"That's strictly medicinal, and you know I don't smoke when I'm working."

Mai bristled at Dale's outrage at her father's suggestion they might be dating. Emergency room touches and long glances notwithstanding, she knew where she stood with ever dating Dale Miller. She studied the dusty toes of her skate shoes.

"No? Well that's a damn shame." Eli brushed his hands together.

"She's the big renovation I told you about. She's staying with us and she's teaching Noah to cook. Didn't Thomas tell you?"

"If it doesn't involve numbers that boy doesn't tell me nothing. Well then, Mai Li, who is not dating my daughter, what can I do for you?" His gaze landed on Mai's bandaged hand. "Break your hand in a bar fight?"

Mai guffawed. "Nah. Lost a fight with a kitchen knife. Noah said you had a two-burner camp stove. Would you be willing to lend it to me?"

"Going camping? Dale loves to camp."

Dale groaned and hid her face in her hands. "Give it a rest, Dad."

"I want to use it for the farmer's market to set up an omelet stand."

"I heard the crepe lady took off back to France. Pity. They were the best crepes I've ever had. You make crepes?" He peered at Mai over the rims of his glasses. His eyes were a piercing blue.

"I can. But I make better omelets." Mai shifted back and forth on her feet. "I can rent it or buy it."

Eli rubbed his hand over his beard. "I'm seeing a special lady right now. Would you trade me a fancy dinner for the use of the cooktop? You wouldn't have to stay to serve. Just drop it off and then make yourself scarce." He waggled his eyebrows.

"Done." Mai held out her hand and Eli shook it. "You do text?"

Eli straightened. "I'm old but I'm not dead." He pulled his phone from the back pocket of his jeans.

"Let's trade numbers. Send me the date you want me to cook and a list of what you want me to make for your seduction dinner."

"Oh my God, you're as bad as he is." Dale jingled her car keys.

Eli tilted his head toward the door of the shop. "Cooktop's in the shed." He led them out to a tin-roofed outbuilding. He pulled a clump of keys from his pocket and sorted through them for the key to the rusty lock. Swinging the door wide, he gestured to a tarp in the corner. "It's under there." He turned to Dale. "Go get your truck so you don't have to carry it so far."

Dale turned to go and turned back. She shot a hard look at her father. "Behave, Dad." She stalked away from them.

Mai stared at her and wondered at her anger. If her mother had been accepting at all when she came out, Mai would have done cartwheels. And never left.

"Don't let her anger put you off." Eli's quiet whisper startled Mai from her thoughts.

She turned to him. He had taken his glasses off and was cleaning them on his shirt.

"She's been burnt. More than once. That idiot she married did her a favor when he run off. But she's not fared much better with women. My girl might be a brilliant contractor but she's lousy at picking partners. After the last one." He grimaced. "After she bailed with Dale's money, she's shut herself off."

Mai shrugged. "We're not dating. You saw how she reacted when you even suggested it."

Eli put his glasses back on. "I know my daughter. She's mad because I said what she's wishing for and is too afraid to want."

A cloud of dust and the crunch of tires on dirt announced the arrival of the truck.

Mai chewed her lip. "I think she's seeing someone right now."

"No one she's bought out here."

"We needed the cooktop."

"Uh huh. Or let stay in her home. Or let anywhere near her sons."

Mai turned over all the things Eli had said. A spark of hope flickered in her chest. She turned and watched Dale as she lowered the pickup's tailgate and spread a tarp over the bed.

Eli's broad palm rested on her shoulder and he squeezed lightly. "Come on. Let's get this thing loaded."

*

"Want some popcorn?" Noah stood and stretched.

"Yes, please."

"You want another beer to go with it?"

"Noah Jerome, I can't believe you don't already know the answer to that."

"Got it." Noah picked up Dale's empty beer bottle from the end table and carried it with him to the kitchen. Dale shifted on the couch and tucked her legs up under her as she searched for *Fight Club*.

The back door banged open and she startled, dropping the remote. The rich murmur of Mai's voice made her nipples half hard. *Why? Why does she have to be so fucking sexy?* Dale snatched up the remote, grabbed a couch pillow, and clutched it to her chest, worried her traitorous nipples would betray her.

Mai strode into the living room. Her hair was slicked back and her skin glistened. Dale swallowed hard and forced herself to look away from Mai's muscular thighs displayed by her running shorts.

"Hey, Noah invited me to watch *Fight Club*. You okay with it?"

"Why wouldn't I be?"

"I wanted to make sure I wasn't crashing any family time."

"You're welcome to watch with us, and we should be asking you."

"Why?" Mai swiped a hand over her forehead and the beads of sweat there.

"We're sitting on your bed." Dale gestured to the couch.

Mai laughed. "It's fine. I need to shower. Save me some popcorn?"

"Sure."

Mai walked away. Dale stared, openly admiring the way the shimmery fabric moved over Mai's ass. She watched until Mai made the turn into Dale's bedroom and she could no longer see her.

She closed her eyes and rested her head on the back of the couch. The scent of hot oil and popcorn filled the air as Noah worked his magic in the kitchen. *What the fuck am I going to do? I can't do this. Not again.* Dale held tight to the pillow and gave over to all her fears. *Why is she so worried about money? And where is Yvonne?* Mai hadn't said and Dale was too much of a coward to ask. Dale envied Yvonne, as she imagined what it would be like to have a partner as who worked as hard as Mai, someone as considerate of Yvonne's needs now and in the future.

"Mom?" Noah's voice startled her, and Dale opened her eyes to her son holding a giant bowl of popcorn and a dark-brown bottle of beer.

"Thanks, sweetie." Dale took the beer and avoided Noah's eyes. Her youngest son was sensitive to her moods, had no filter, and if there was anything she didn't want to talk about right now it was her feelings.

"You wanna wait for Mai?" Noah plopped down on the couch next to her.

Dale took a long pull on her beer. "Yes."

"Me too." Noah stuffed a large handful of popcorn in his mouth.

*

Dale's long legs draped in soft black lounge pants did nothing for Mai's concentration. Grateful for Noah's constant chatter as they watched *Fight Club* for what must be the hundredth time in Mai's life, she sipped her beer and took advantage of the dim light to study Dale's profile. Dale's soft laugher as she watched Helena Bonham Carter's antics on the screen melted Mai's heart.

Dale's hair was held back by a wide black band and the lustrous strands gathered at the back of her neck. The elegant nape of her neck begged for kisses and Mai's mouth watered as she imagined kissing her way along the smooth column of her throat and nibbling her delicate earlobe. Mai had caught sight of her neat toes, painted a pale shade of pink, before Dale tucked them under her. Now Dale's feet were tucked up on the couch and her shins pressed against Mai's thigh and hip, as they all crowded together on the couch.

Mai's body burned with Dale's closeness. Didn't she notice? Maybe she did. Maybe that's why she had become more relaxed around Mai. Had even taken to getting up earlier to eat the breakfast Mai prepared for her. *No. She likes my cooking. It's not me. She doesn't like me like that.* Her mind flitted back to Dale's dating profile. *She's looking to hook up. If I had her once and nothing more it would kill me.* A wave of guilt washed over Mai. *And Noah. He would get his hopes up for nothing.*

Mai loved Noah, liked she loved Yvonne. He had a zeal for cooking that matched her own. It was like having a little brother. The one Mai had begged for as a child. It was years before she understood Yvonne's birth had almost killed her mother.

She had planned on sitting on the opposite end of the couch with Noah between them but somehow Noah had managed to have her between him and his mother. His unsubtle attempts at matchmaking between her and Dale were sweet and infuriating.

Mai was not stupid enough to believe Dale had not noticed. She flushed, unable to avert her gaze when Dale leaned over to pick up her beer. Her loose V-neck shirt pulled open, offering an unfettered glimpse of the smooth curves of her breasts.

Noah's guffaw at the action on the screen startled Mai and she refocused her gaze on the television.

"I don't care how many times I've seen this. It still makes me laugh." Noah held out the bowl of popcorn and shook it, rattling the unpopped kernels. "You want I should make some more?"

"I'm good." Mai leaned back and stretched her arms. "Mom?"

"I've had plenty. You want us to pause the movie?"

"Nah. I could recite it." Noah shuffled out of the living room carrying the popcorn bowl and his pop and their empty beer bottles.

Mai chewed her lip. The silence between her and Dale was deafening. She could hear Noah's movements in the kitchen as he cleaned up.

"How'd your date go the other night?" Mai knotted her fingers together.

Dale grimaced. "I've had better times at the dentist."

Mai covered her mouth to hide her grin. "That bad?"

"Voice like nails on a chalkboard and vapid. I asked her to tell me something about herself and she said, 'I like white wine because it has less calories.' After that I faked a headache and asked for the check."

Mai chewed her lip. "It's rough out there. It's hard to tell anything by a profile."

Dale pursed her lips. "That it is. It's better if you can meet someone, you know, and then figure out if you want to ask them out. Not much of a dating pool here."

Mai frowned. "I guess not."

"I mean. Well, of course. I didn't mean..." Dale bolted off the couch and shoved her feet into her slippers. "Is that the time? Damn, I have an early day tomorrow." She moved away from the couch. "Noah! I'm going to bed and you should too. It's a school night."

Noah peeked around the archway. "Got it. There's like ten minutes left in the movie, Mom. I'll go up then."

Dale waved at the two of them before she hurried down the hall toward her bedroom.

Noah sat down as the credits rolled, giggling at the outtakes. "The outtakes are epic." He leaned back and spread his arms along the back of the couch. "What'd you guys talk about? Mom looked freaked when she left."

"Dating." Mai pulled her feet up on the couch and wrapped her arms around her thighs, hugging her legs to her chest.

Noah's eyes brightened. "For real?"

"Not like that." Mai hated the way his eyes shuttered. "Sorry. I didn't mean to sound harsh. Your mom had a bad date last weekend and she was telling me about it. And how there's not much of a 'dating pool' in the town."

Noah looked away. "That sucks."

It did. And that was okay. She hadn't come here to find a partner. But it stung to know she wasn't even on Dale's radar.

*

The bedroom door closed with a sharp snick and Dale slumped against it. She groaned as she thought about her hurtful comment to Mai on the couch and the expression in Mai's face. *Way to go, Miller. Now she thinks you don't even consider her date material. Fuck, what if she thinks it's a race thing? Or a butch thing? Oh fuck.*

She stormed into her bathroom, yanked the hairband from her hair, and tossed it on the counter. After taking her toothbrush from the stand, she pulled the toothpaste tube from the drawer. She squeezed the tube hard and overshot her toothbrush. "Fuck."

After using her finger to scrape the blue-and-green striped gel off the sink, Dale wiped it on the bristles. She wet her finger and washed away the rest of the toothpaste as she brushed her teeth. She kept her gaze focused on the white porcelain of the sink and avoided the glass, too annoyed to even look at herself.

Dale grimaced when she thought of the number of dating profiles she had seen on the Hit Me Up app stating "no butches, no blacks, no Asians, no Hispanic." She automatically swiped left on those profiles, no matter how much the other bits of the bio might appeal. It was an automatic pass on her list of criteria. And now after her tactless comment she might have given Mai the impression she was a jerk and a racist. Dale finished brushing her teeth. A quick scrub of her face with the washcloth and she was ready for bed.

In her room she could hear the muffled sounds of Noah and Mai talking in the living room. She crept to the door. Even with her ear pressed to the smooth wood she couldn't make out what they were saying. Noah's rumbling baritone faded, and Dale waited until she heard his heavy tread on the stairs before she opened the door to her room.

With light steps she walked back to the living room. Mai was lying on the couch under a blanket, her head propped up on pillows. The end table lamp was on low and a worn paperback blocked Dale's view of Mai's face.

Dale stopped with her hand on the archway wall. "Mai?"

Mai jerked. Her paperback fell to the floor and she stared at Dale. "You scared the hell out of me. The damn clown is about to get another kid." She pressed her hand to her chest over her heart. "What?"

Dale walked to the couch and scooped up the paperback. "I'm sorry." She passed the paperback to Mai. "I'm sorry about before too." At Mai's quizzical expression she continued. "I don't want you to think I meant you when I was talking about the standard of the dating pool."

"It's fine." Mai glanced down at her book. Her hands were white knuckled where she gripped the cover.

"No, it's not. I think anyone would be lucky to date you."

Mai's eyebrows rose and held Dale's gaze.

"And folks who don't date people because of who they are, or how they look are ignorant." Dale crossed her arms over her chest.

"Thanks for clearing that up." Mai's crooked grin fanned the fire in Dale's heart to blaze. "I'm still a little tender. Charlene went out of her way to try and change how I am." She sighed. "I don't think she liked anything about me but my money."

"I know how that feels." Dale pushed her hair back with one hand, shoving aside memories of Molly. "Well, Charlene's an idiot." Dale held Mai's gaze for a beat. "Good night."

"See you at breakfast." Mai picked up her book and opened it.

"Sleep well." Dale walked back toward her bedroom. She stopped before she reached the hall and turned to find Mai staring at her. Their eyes locked and Dale's heart rate sped up. Mai's gaze burned and a tendril of desire twisted its way through Dale's body. The urge to return to the couch, to press Mai back on to the cushions and kiss her, to lay over her and have her long lean body under her own stifled her. She twisted the hem of her T-shirt in her hands.

"Good night," she called over her shoulder as she hustled away to the safety of her room.

Dale shut the door to her room and collapsed on her mattress. She scooted up, lifted her hips, and wiggled under the covers. With both hands she held the comforter tight to her chest. Thighs wet with want, her pulse loud in her ears, she replayed the scene in the living room in her head. Right or wrong she wanted Mai. She drew in a ragged breath. And if Mai's expression was any indication Mai wanted her. No mistaking the hunger in her eyes.

Dale relaxed her grip on the sheets and closed her eyes. A random collage of images of Mai flashed through her mind. The sexy curve of her lips when she smiled, the way she was attentive when they talked, as if Dale was the only person in the world she wanted to listen to, and the way she was with Noah.

Noah had blossomed with Mai's tutoring and her cooking lessons. Her caring and confidence had Dale hooked. And what was she going to do about it? Nothing. She was a client. And attached. To Yvonne. Dale had pushed aside jealous feelings more than once as she had caught snippets of Mai's weekly phone calls to Yvonne. *Not for me. She's attached. Or about to be. What about a casual thing? No. Not that way. I'd hate to have the memory and the heartache. Better not to know.*

Dale flopped to her side and drew her legs up, curling in on herself. She wouldn't get Noah's hopes up like that. Or her own.

*

Dale sipped her coffee and studied Mai from under her eyelashes as she and Noah worked on the week's meal plan. She glanced up and Dale shifted her gaze, her face heating.

Mai drew her hand over her hair. "Where do you get your hair cut, Noah?"

Noah pointed his pencil at Dale. "Mom cuts it."

"Really?"

"Guilty." Dale took a bite of her sandwich.

Mai eyed Noah's stylish cut and shifted her gaze back to Dale. "Would you cut mine?"

Dale finished her bite of sandwich. "I'd love to." Mai's raised eyebrow at Dale's enthusiasm made her flush. "I mean if you're okay with a basic cut."

"I'm tired of being shaggy and afraid to cut it myself."

Dale frowned. "Is it curly like Thomas's? Or more wavy like Noah's? If it's like Thomas's I can't do it."

"It's like Noah's when it grows out." Mai leaned back in her seat. "Would you have time today?"

Dale pursed her lips and glanced at the clock. "Hot date?"

Mai avoided her eyes. "It you don't have time it's fine."

"I've got time if we do it now. Promise you won't be upset if it's not perfect?"

"Anything is better than this mess."

Dale stood and carried her dishes to the sink. "I'll get my stuff. Meet me on the porch. Bring a counter stool."

*

Mai sat on the high stool. Dale draped a towel over her shoulders and clipped it in place.

"How do you want me to cut it?"

"Can you do a fade? Like skin on the sides and then longer on top?"

"I'll do my best." Dale rested her palms on Mai's shoulders.

The heat from Dale's body combined with the sensation of her fingers on Mai's shoulder as she combed her fingers through her hair sent a ripple of want through Mai's body. Her nipples hardened with the intimacy of Dale's touch.

Dale started with the clippers. Working carefully, she shaved the sides and back of Mai's head, tapering the cut toward the crown of Mai's head. Mai pressed her lips together and focused on not asking Dale for a date. Dale worked silently and the buzz of the clippers was the only sound on the porch.

After Dale's apology last evening and the expression on her face when she turned to look back at her, Mai had struggled with her desire to follow her down the hall to her bedroom. In her dreams, she had opened the door and kneeled at Dale's feet, pressed kisses to the top of her manicured toes, and begged her for what she wanted. What she wished they both wanted.

Dale placed the clippers aside. She misted Mai's hair before she started working on the top and front. Mai closed her eyes as the bits of hair fell.

"Hold still." Dale brushed the loose hair from Mai's face with a soft brush. "All good."

Mai opened her eyes.

Dale passed a hand mirror to Mai. "Is this short enough?" She held another mirror behind Mai for her to check her reflection.

Mai lowered the glass and turned to Dale. "It's fine."

"So, your date will approve?"

"Do you?" The words burbled from Mai's mouth before she could stop them.

Dale lowered the mirror she was holding. "What?"

"I don't have a date, other than you invited me to come to the brew pub on Saturday." The words tumbled from Mai's mouth in a rush.

Dale's hands rested on Mai's shoulders a moment before she brushed her thumb over the short hairs at the back of Mai's neck. "I like it this way."

Mai's breath caught and she stilled under Dale's touch.

"Mom, Mrs. Haskin's on the phone about her she-shed," Noah shouted from inside the house.

"I'll be right there." Dale stepped back. "I have to take that."

Mai hopped off the stool. "I'll clean up. Thank you."

"My pleasure." Dale held Mai's gaze a beat before she left.

Mai pulled the towel off and shook it out. Three swipes with the broom and she had cleaned the porch. After packing up Dale's kit she ran her hand over her hair. Tiny bits of hair stuck to her palm as she touched the spot on her neck where Dale's fingers had been. Hope, reckless and ridiculous, filled her heart.

Chapter Twelve

"Noah, slow down." Dale's high-pitched warning made Mai grit her teeth.

The back of Noah's neck flushed red. "I got it, Mom."

He pulled into the last space in the tightly packed parking lot. He shoved the gearshift into park. "I don't know if this being the designated driver thing is worth it if you're going to yell at me."

Dale swept her hand through her hair. "Sorry."

Mai opened her door and opened Dale's door before she offered her hand.

Dale stared at Mai's hand long enough a flush spread over Mai's face. She placed her hand in Mai's and let her help her down from the truck.

A stiff summer breeze fluttered Dale's jade-green wrap dress around her thighs.

"Come on. Grandpa's probably freaking out thinking we're not coming."

Dale let go of Mai's hand and walked ahead of her between the cars. Mai followed Dale and Noah through the heavy glass doors into the bar. The scent of stale beer and fried foods greeted them.

The hostess smiled broadly at Dale. "Hey sister, we haven't seen you in an age." She picked up a stack of menus and waved them forward. "Your pop's here already."

They picked their way through the tables packed with families. Little kids in high chairs sat next to grandparents and the din of piped-in '80s rock added to the cacophony of the chain brew pub.

A waitress passed them with a round tray loaded with beers in various shades. Mai's nose caught the rich caramel scent of hops and grains brewed to perfection. She'd not had a decent stout in ages, and the creamy foam-topped nut-brown liquid in the glass made her anxious get to their table and place her order.

Eli waved to them as they approached the table. The rubber bands holding his braided beard were fluorescent-green tonight and his bright-red T-shirt proudly proclaimed "you can't scare me I have two daughters" in white script. Dale leaned down and kissed her father's cheek before she sat next to him. Noah fist-bumped his grandfather and took a seat to his mom. Mai sat in the chair next to Eli and picked up her menu.

"I ordered us some fried pickles." Eli sipped a blond beer and then tilted his glass toward Mai. "This Belgian is good."

Dale pursed her lips. "I'm not sure what I want. They've changed over to their summer brews."

Mai looked over the long list of beers offered. "Want to share a flight?"

"Sounds good." Dale laid her menu aside.

Eli lifted his chin at Noah and pulled a rubber-banded deck of UNO cards from his back pocket. "You ready to get beat?"

Noah grinned, laced his fingers together, and stretched them outward. "Bring it, old man."

A stout man arrived out of breath and lugging a laptop case. "Sorry. Had some stuff to take care of at work before I could leave." He leaned down and kissed Dale's cheek. He held his hand out. "You must be Mai. Thomas." He was shorter than Noah, his frame packed with muscles a power lifter would envy. His dark-brown hair spread out in wiry curls. He grinned at Mai, his light-brown eyes twinkling behind wire-rimmed glasses with thick lenses. "Nice to meet you."

Mai shook his hand. "You as well."

After stowing his briefcase under the table, he sat next to her. "Did you order yet?"

"Just got here."

Eli dealt the cards to everyone. He paused at Mai. "I'm assuming you play?"

"Not in years, but yes."

Thomas rolled his eyes. "We haven't even got our drinks yet, Granddad."

"Time and Eli Miller wait for no one. Ya in or out?"

Thomas rapped the tabletop with his knuckles. "I'm in."

The server loomed over the table. He was tall, with sandy-blond hair and a trimmed scruff of beard, and his too-small T-shirt pulled tight over his broad chest and biceps. His heavy cologne made Mai wrinkle her nose.

He positioned himself behind Dale's chair and rested his thick hand on the back of it. Mai noticed the stiffening of Dale's posture. A black-and-gold tag declared his name as "Ethan."

"Hey, y'all, do you know what you want?" Ethan's gaze landed on Dale's cleavage. Noah, Eli, and Thomas gave their orders and Ethan scratched them down on his order sheet. He leaned down close to Dale, invading her space, and spoke in what he must have believed to be a seductive tone. "And how about you, my lovely Ms. Miller? What can I tempt you with tonight?"

Dale shifted her chair and a flash of anger crossed her face as she gripped the edge of the table.

Mai leaned back in her chair and spoke loudly. "She and I are having the beer flight. What are your specials?"

Ethan glanced at Mai and a frown flashed over his face before he smoothed his features. He straightened and shifted on his feet, his gaze tracking back to Dale's cleavage. "Uh, they're listed in the front"—he hooked his thumb over his shoulder—"on the chalkboard."

Mai tapped the table with her finger to draw his attention. "I'm not at the front. And I can't see the chalkboard from here."

Ethan smirked and raked his gaze over Mai. "Did you just get off the boat? Folks from here know to read the board when they come in. You can read English, right?"

Mai clenched her fist under the table at his unsubtle insinuation. "Think you could tell me what they are? That is, if you can stop looking down my friend's dress long enough to concentrate?"

Dale raised her eyebrows and stared at Mai for a beat before she shifted her gaze to Ethan.

Eli slapped his hand on the table and punched Mai's shoulder gently. "I knew I liked you."

Ethan's face flushed. "I wasn't..." He withered under Mai's glare. "I'll go find out."

Dale frowned at Mai. "I don't need to be saved."

Mai crossed her arms over her chest. "I wasn't saving you. He was being creepy and disrespectful. It's not okay to stare at someone's breasts like he was. Maybe he'll think twice before he does it again."

Eli sipped his beer. "We gonna play or what?"

Mai picked up her hand and sorted them by color and number. She studied Dale's face over the top of her cards.

Pushing aside her anger over Ethan's comments, she forced herself to focus on the hand Eli had dealt her. Icy-cold liquid spilled down her back and she leaped to her feet. Sticky soda ran down her arm and she dropped her cards on the table.

Ethan smirked as he deposited the glass and what was left of Thomas's soda on the table.

"Sorry about that." He could not have sounded less sincere if he'd tried. "Our specials are fried chicken and fried green tomatoes served with house bread and a meatloaf dinner with mashed potatoes and fresh peas. No rice today."

Mai lifted her wet shirt from her back with one hand and balled the other into a fist. Unwilling to start a fight in the middle of a restaurant filled with small children and their families, she counted to ten in her head.

"That make you feel like a man, Ethan?" Dale's acid tone cut through Mai's anger.

Ethan backed up as Dale rounded the table, her face contorted into a thunderous glare. She gestured at the surrounding tables now gone quiet as they watched the scene unfold. "Showing off for these people? Get your manager."

"You mean my mom?" Ethan smirked again and cocked his eyebrow.

Dale stepped closer and jutted out her chin. "Get her. Now."

He turned on his heel and left them. Dale reached out and rested her hand on Mai's arm. "I'm sorry."

"You're sorry? He's the one who's going to be sorry." Mai pointed to the kitchen door Ethan had gone through. "He has no idea who I know. He's clueless. His mom's the manager, big fucking deal. I know the owner of the entire chain. He and his mom are going to be out of their jobs as soon as I get off the phone." Mai wiped her hand on her jeans.

Dale sniffed and lifted her chin. "Let me handle this. His mom's not a bad person. She's had a time with him since her husband died."

"Fine." Mai sat down. The sticky soda drying on the skin of her back made her itch. She grabbed a wad of paper napkins and attempted to dry herself off. It wasn't fine. It wasn't fine at all, but she'd let Dale handle it for now.

Dale left the table and walked to the bar. She talked with the bartender a moment. The burly man frowned as he looked over Dale's shoulder at their table. He tilted his head toward the rear of the bar and Dale walked toward the door he had indicated.

Eli peeled apart Mai's soggy stack of UNO cards and dabbed at them with his napkin before he laid them out on the table. "Let her do it. Kid's an idiot."

Mai shifted in her seat. "If I'd been a dude, he wouldn't have pulled that crap."

"If you'd been a dude, Dale wouldn't have invited you to join us. Simmer down and play." Eli lifted his chin at her. "Let's not let that jackass ruin our night."

Noah flipped over the top card from the stack, a blue eight. "Grandad's right. Mom always says don't let the bullies win." His mouth pulled into a grimace. "Ethan was a senior when I was a freshman. He and his crew used to stuff me in my locker all the time.

"Until Seth and I handed him his ass one afternoon." Thomas guffawed. "He never touched Noah again."

Mai huffed out a breath. "He's got a history of being a bully?"

Eli laid down a red eight and placed it squarely on the pile started by Noah. "Only reason he's not in a detention facility is his uncle's a deputy. No one will hire him. He's only got a job because his mother's the manager here."

Mai chewed her lip. "Bad seed." She flipped a red skip card onto the pile.

Thomas pulled his glasses off, cleaned them on his shirt, and groaned. "Dang it, skip cards in the first round is never good."

Mai's mouth was dry, and she contemplated going to the bar and retrieving their beer flight herself.

Dale's warm hand on her sticky shoulder made her start. "Our meals are on the house."

Mai turned her head to look into Dale's eyes. "And Ethan?"

Dale pursed her lips. "Ethan won't be serving us, or anyone else tonight." She squeezed Mai's shoulder once and then returned to her seat.

"It's your turn, Mom." Noah shifted in his chair. "Mai skipped Thomas."

"Oh, that's never good early." She sat down and gazed at Mai over her cards.

Mai's thoughts roiled. *So, business as usual. A racist ass dumps soda down my back and we go on playing cards?* Rage welled up. Cold, unvented rage.

She pushed back from the table and stood up. "I'm sorry. I need to go." The group looked at her as one. Mai shifted her gaze to each one of their faces. "A free meal and change of server isn't going to cut it for me. He made racist comments and assaulted me. I'm out. I'll get a taxi home." She walked away from the table, frustrated by their lack of understanding, and furious anger swept over her. *Why the fuck did I think this town would be different from when I was growing up?*

*

Dale caught up with Mai in the parking lot. "Mai!"

Mai turned to her. "You don't have to end your evening." She scuffed her shoe over the gravel and shoved her hands into her pockets.

"I don't understand." Dale stepped close and placed her hand on Mai's forearm. "Please talk to me. I want to."

Mai skewered her gaze. "I don't need a white savior. I'm mad at myself for tolerating his behavior and mad at you for not getting it. Free dinner is supposed to make up for what he said and implied? We go on about our night and pretend it's all good? My family has lived in this county since the 1800s, at least as long as his family. And yet because of my appearance he feels entitled to say and do the things he did? And no one makes a big deal out of it? Fuck that. And fuck him." Mai yanked away from Dale's touch.

Dale lowered her chin to her chest. "I'm sorry. What should I have done?"

"Let me handle it. Let me fight my own battles. If I need backup, I'll let you know. Hold space for me, but don't take over."

Dale clasped her hands in front of her dress. "I won't do it again."

Mai blew out a breath. "I need some time and some space. Is it okay if I take the truck, and come back to pick you up when you want to leave?" She looked down and away from Dale.

"Sure." Dale studied the dejected set of Mai's shoulders. She stepped closer to her and rested her fingertips on her forearm. "Would you like company? We don't have to talk but I'm a good listener if you want to talk. Or do you want to be alone? I understand if you do."

"I don't want to take you away from family night." Mai pursed her lips.

Dale heart ached at the sadness she saw in Mai's eyes. "Thomas can bring Noah home. Let me tell them what's up."

Mai nodded her silent agreement. Dale handed her the keys to the truck and hurried back to the restaurant. At the table, Eli was in the process of shuffling the cards while Noah and Thomas argued over the last fried pickle.

"Hey, Dad?"

Eli looked up. "Yes, daughter dear. Let me guess. You want to comfort your friend in her hour of need?" He set the cards aside. "Am I right?"

Dale flushed. "For fuck's sake, Dad. Ethan was an idiot and I doubled down on it by not letting her handle it." She turned to Thomas. "Will you bring Noah home?"

"Sure, Mom." Thomas's brow wrinkled. "Be careful." Dale raised her eyebrow and Thomas flushed. "I mean... Ah hell, Mom. She seems nice an' all but..."

Dale pinned her son in place with her gaze. "She's not Molly. Not even close. And I don't appreciate the concern."

Thomas ducked his head. "Got it."

Eli waved "See ya. Your woman's waiting."

Dale rolled her eyes. "She's not my anything, Dad."

"Not yet." Eli lifted his beer and took a large sip.

"How are you getting home, Dad?" Dale failed to keep the worried tone out of her voice.

"The fabulous Ms. Zettler is picking me up after her shift at the brush factory." Eli waggled his bushy eyebrows.

Dale leaned down and hugged his shoulder. "Be safe."

She turned to go, and he caught her arm and tugged her close. "I love you, kiddo."

"I know, Dad, I know." Dale slipped her arm through the strap of her purse and left.

*

Mai drove out of the parking lot and flicked the button for the headlights. The glittering blacktop road stretched before her and she drove north. Dale had said nothing when she returned from the restaurant and climbed into the truck and Mai was grateful for the quiet.

Charlene had never understood, not even tried to understand the racism and homophobia Mai faced. Never believed Mai when she related the stories of the latest micro-aggressions and the more brazen racist episodes that happened to her on the regular. She'd even gone as far as suggest Mai "soften" her look and use makeup to not appear so "ethnic."

Why did it take me catching her banging the producer for me to get she never loved me, just my money? The road forked and Mai turned left, not caring where she went, needing to drive, to get away from the black cloud of anger chasing her. Fields crowded against the sides of the road and the evening deepened.

Dale shifted in her seat. "I truly am sorry. I've only had to deal with homophobia, and not much of that because people never think I'm queer because I have kids."

"And how you present." Mai kept her gaze fixed on the road.

"Exactly. No one ever thinks I'm queer even when I show up in flannel and jeans."

"Do you know what the kids on the high school basketball team nicknamed me?"

"No."

"Blackie Chan. Because of my mom. They thought it was hilarious. And you know what kills me? I went along with it. Let them get away with it." Mai's gut twisted. "I didn't say anything. The first time my folks came to see me play and heard it, they never came back to watch a game again." She banged her palm on the steering wheel. "And tonight, that asshat, Ethan, was every fucker who has disrespected me in my life. He gets a reprimand, gets sent home from work, and I get an ulcer because I let him get away with it. But not this time."

"What are you going to do?" Dale twisted her hands together.

"I'm going to contact my friend. Let him know what kind of bullshit is going down at this restaurant. He'll take it from there. What do you think would have happened if I had done something in the restaurant?"

Dale shrugged. "I don't know."

"Right. You think if I had started something when the cops showed up Ethan would have been in trouble? The blond-haired blue-eyed kid who 'accidentally' spilled a drink? I would have been seen as unreasonable and oversensitive. I'm betting I would have been invited to leave that fine establishment." Mai fisted her hand and banged the roof of the truck cab. "Fuck me, but I wanted to punch his simpering face. I looked around at all those families and the kids and I couldn't do it. Kids don't need to see that." Mai glanced at Dale before she returned her gaze to the road. "I was half hoping he'd been waiting in the parking lot ready to start something I could finish. Part of me wanted to go looking for him to make a point." Mai waved her hand. "But I just got use of this hand back and I don't want to risk busting my knuckles up or going to jail. Or worse."

She turned into the gravel parking lot of a roadhouse. The parking lot was full of trucks with hunting racks and toolboxes. The low dark building had blacked-out windows. A squat post with a gaudy neon sign that flashed "cold beer" and "live music" illuminated the short walk to the door of the bar. Mai turned the car off and pointed to the bar. "You ever been here?"

Dale turned and faced Mai. "No. And we shouldn't go in. Unless you want to get into a fight. Not that I blame you for wanting to punch someone." She glanced down at her wedge sandals. "If I'd known you wanted to start some shit, I'd have worn my boots."

Mai lifted her chin. "See. Here's the thing. You could go in. You might have to tell a few of the boys to get lost, that you weren't interested in dating, but you wouldn't have to worry about some asshole telling you to go back to the country you came from. Or calling you a dyke. Or waiting in the dark to show you what you're missing by being a lesbian. You get it. Or you wouldn't be worried about us going in. But you've never had to think about it before."

Dale sighed. "You're right. You must be exhausted thinking about it all the time. Trying to stay safe."

Mai shrugged. "I got spoiled by living in a big city. It's still there but it's more remote and you can insulate yourself if you work at it. But it's always there, a low-level hum of alertness all the fucking time. It's more subtle. They don't call you dyke to your face. You just don't get the call back, or the job, or they ask you to dress differently, or wear makeup."

Dale leaned back in her seat. "It's worse here?"

"What do you think?"

Dale shrunk back from Mai's anger. "Stupid question. Forgive me."

"Sorry. I'm not mad at you. You're trying. Most folks don't want to talk about it. It makes them uncomfortable."

"I want to know you, Mai. Noah thinks you're amazing." Dale rested her chin on her chest. "So do I."

Mai's traitorous heart lifted with Dale's confession. *It doesn't mean anything. Calm down.*

"Noah's wonderful." Mai shifted in her seat and tapped her fingers on the wheel. She swallowed around the hard knot in her dry throat and ran her tongue over her lip. "Damn, we never got to try our beer flight."

Dale reached over and rested her hand on Mai's knee. The warmth of her palm shot tingles of desire through Mai. Her anger morphed into need and she glanced at Dale's face.

"I've got a six-pack in the refrigerator in the basement at home." Dale met Mai's gaze. "If you're interested. It's not top of the line but it's decent." Her eyes glittered. "The porch is lovely this time of night."

Fireflies flicked at the edge of the parking lot. Mai shivered with the huskiness of Dale's voice. Mai leaned closer, drawn by the invitation in her voice. Dale's lips parted and the subtle notes of her perfume wove around them. Dale's eyes went wide before her gaze settled on Mai's mouth. Mai fell hard into the dark depths of Dale's golden-brown eyes as her fingers tightened on her knee.

"I'd like that." Mai leaned closer, wanting to close the distance, wanting to kiss Dale until they were both desperate for air and clinging to each other. The flare of headlights from a Jeep turning into the parking lot with Mötley Crüe's "Girls, Girls, Girls" blaring from its open windows startled them. Mai jerked back, placed both hands on the wheel, and stifled her groan of disappointment.

Dale drew her hand away and settled back in her seat. "Me too."

Chapter Thirteen

Twelve weeks. Four since the night they had spent drinking beer on the porch after a near kiss in Dale's truck. Dale had relived that moment at least once a day since it had happened. Mai had been about to kiss her. She knew it. And Dale had wanted her to. Wanted to do much more than kiss. But Mai had been careful since then to not be alone with Dale.

No mixing business and pleasure. It was for the best. Dale knew it. But the heat of that moment and the fire in Mai's eyes and the way her thigh had tensed under Dale's fingertips haunted her.

In the three months since Mai had moved into Dale's home, Dale's life had settled down from the eye-bleeding chaos of her trying to run her business and manage her home. Seth was back in his basement room. Noah was doing well in summer school. Thomas was two courses away from finishing with his accounting degree.

Dale had cleared out part of her closet and they had brought a spare dresser from the attic for Mai's clothes. Cartoon animals and race car decals covered it, souvenirs from its time as a fixture in Seth and Thomas's room. Mai was meticulous in everything she did, and her presence forced Dale to make more of an effort to keep her bedroom tidy.

Dale's world went from dinners consisting of whatever she could throw together when she got home from working twelve hours, or whatever food experiment Noah had come up with to various delectable dinners Mai and Noah had created together. She shook her head, trying to clear the memories of tapioca soup, a failed attempt by Noah before Mai arrived that they both still laughed about.

She unlaced her boots and toed them off before setting them on the mat on the porch. The scent of saffron wafted from the kitchen through the screen door and she inhaled. Her mouth watered.

Noah was at the stove stirring a saucepan. Mai was perched on a kitchen stool at the bar separating the kitchen from the dining area.

"What's cooking?" Dale squeezed Noah's shoulder. "Smells fantastic."

"Vegetable biryani. There's eggplant masala too." Noah lifted the lid on a casserole dish. "Mai's going out. Seth's out with Thomas. It's just us."

A flash of annoyance shot through Dale before she caught herself. "Will it hold? I want to shower before dinner."

"Yes. The best thing about many Indian dishes is they will hold beautifully." Mai slid off the high-backed bar stool. "I might be late."

Dale slid her gaze over Mai's pressed baby-blue tailored shirt tucked into tight black jeans. "Don't worry, I won't bother to wait up."

Mai's raised eyebrows let Dale know she'd failed to keep her annoyance out of her voice. She walked away briskly, not sure of what else she could say that wouldn't make it worse.

Dale closed the bathroom door and locked it and leaned her forehead against the white-painted wood a moment. *What the hell is wrong with me? They must have an open relationship. So of course she's going to date. Why wouldn't she? And why am I not dating?* She turned the taps on and started the shower to let the water warm up as she stripped off her clothes. Dale stepped into the shower and turned her back to the hot spray. Soothing jets of water beat against her tight shoulder muscles. *She can do anything she wants. It's not like she's mine or anything.*

Her gut churned as she thought about her last disaster of a date. Skylar. Who couldn't take a hint and was still calling and texting Dale. Another in a long string of unsatisfying dinners and even less satisfying sex in most cases. But if she were honest it was because none of the women she had dated had even a tenth of Mai's easy charm. And now some other woman was going to spend the evening with Mai.

Dale scrubbed her hands over her face when she imagined how Mai's evening might end. Hot anger settled in her belly. *Why not me? Because you put her off. Because you made it clear. No mixing sex and business. And now someone else is going to be all up in Mai's sexy business. Damn it.*

Her stomach growled and she cut her shower short. After pulling on a pair of sweatpants and her favorite T-shirt, Dale picked up her phone off the dresser. Three taps later she was scrolling through Hit Me Up. She gasped when Mai's charming smile lit up her screen. Her thumb hovered over her profile as her entire body begged her to swipe right before her brain interfered and she swiped left. Three profiles later she landed on Badbutchone. She skimmed her profile. Her cocky smile and the bespoke suit she wore in her photo attracted Dale. A classic butch and likely candidate for a hookup. Dale swiped right. The scent of dinner made her mouth water. She chewed her lip while she tapped out a message to Badbutchone.

"Mom! Hurry up, the chapatis are gonna be cold," Noah called from the kitchen.

Dale tossed her phone on the bed and hustled to the kitchen.

*

Dale stirred her drink with her straw and attempted to focus on what Barbara was saying. *Barbara. Why the fuck did I swipe right? No matter how thirsty I am no way I'm fucking this self-important idiot.* The low light in the restaurant made it difficult for Dale to see Barbara's eyes as she droned on about some big business deal she was concocting. The annoying humblebrag tone of Barbara's voice set Dale's teeth on edge. Her mind drifted as she crafted her excuse to not go home with Barbara.

She might be cute but she's arrogant as fuck. Boring as hell. And not Mai. Damn it. Dale sighed and sipped her bourbon and ginger ale. *Nope. Not Mai. Why did I think this would make it better? Fuck me, better to go home and rub one out alone than go home with this asshole.*

The brush of Barbara's fingertips over the back of her hand made Dale jerk away from her touch.

Barbara frowned. "Sorry." The server dropped off the bill jacket and Barbara swept it off the table. She raked her gaze over Dale's breasts before she brought her gaze back to her eyes. "Allow me."

The smugness of her tone and blatant leer detonated Dale's simmering anger. She gripped the edge of the table so she didn't slap Barbara's face. "No. We'll split it." The unspoken undercurrent of what Barbara expected in return for the dinner made Dale's skin crawl.

"It would be my pleasure." Barbara pulled a black credit card from her pocket and tucked into the bill jacket and placed it on the table.

"No." Dale slid the bill over to her side of the table and tucked two twenty-dollar bills into the black folder. She picked up the bill jacket and held it until the server returned.

"Split this, please." Dale lifted her chin at Barbara. "Keep the change from the cash." She stood up and tucked her clutch under her arm. "I'd say it has been charming, but my mother didn't raise a liar."

Barbara looked up at Dale, her eyes wide. "What? What happened? Don't go." She stood and wrapped her fingers around Dale's forearm.

Dale bared her teeth and narrowed her eyes. "Take your hand off me unless you want me to whip your ass right here. And not in a way you would enjoy."

Barbara released Dale's arm and shrank back, her palms raised toward Dale. "What the hell? Was it something I said?"

"You spent the entire evening telling me how great you are and staring at my boobs. If I wanted that kind of interaction, I could have sat the bar for the last hour and a half with some random stranger. Good night."

Dale stalked away, ignoring the stares of the other diners.

At the front of the restaurant she searched her clutch for her keys. She dug them out and gripped them hard. Dale clenched her jaw as she thought about the hour's drive home along back roads to Sikesville and shoved open the door to the restaurant bathroom. Head down, she strode into the bathroom and bumped into a woman coming out. A whiff of Mai's signature cologne filled her senses and she let out a startled squeak as she ran full-on into the woman she'd been fantasizing about for weeks.

*

"Oh hell. I'm sorry." Mai backed up. Her cheeks burned and she plucked her shirt away from her body in an effort to hide the way her nipples had responded to full body contact with Dale.

"You scared the fuck out of me." Dale pressed a hand to her chest. "What are you doing in here? Why didn't you lock the door?"

"I was on my way out." Mai brushed a hand over her hair. "And um—truth? Hiding from my date."

"What?" Dale closed the bathroom door and locked it. "Do you not feel safe?"

Mai smiled at the fierce tone of Dale's voice. "I'm only in danger of being bored to death. And being expected to rock her world for the price of dinner and drinks."

Dale laughed. Mai enjoyed the way her eyes crinkled at the corners and the low rich sound of her laugh. "My date thought drinks were a guarantee of getting in my panties too."

Mai swallowed hard as the vision of Dale in her panties raced through her mind. "I don't know why I thought this date would be any better than any of the others I've been on lately."

Mai stepped back to observe Dale. The shirtwaist dress she wore showed off her pinup figure to perfection and the strapped pumps she wore had Mai wanting to kneel in the bathroom and follow the graceful line of her legs all the way to the tops of her hose and beyond. Sweat trickled between her shoulder blades. "You look terrific."

Dale tilted her head at Mai. "Be that as it may, what's your plan, stud? Hide out here until she decides to leave?"

Mai grinned. "Are you always this sassy?"

"You've lived in my house for three months and you don't know the answer to that?" Dale's gaze settled on Mai. "You want me to give you a boost so you can climb out the window?" A taunting smile curved her full mouth.

Mai stepped closer, the teasing tone of Dale's voice stirring the side of her appreciated pushback from a lover. *Oh damn. Not lovers. I want to be. What the fuck am I going to do?*

Dale leaned toward Mai, her mouth tantalizingly close. "Looks like we both didn't find what we were looking for."

Mai met Dale's gaze. "I don't know about that."

"Oh yeah?"

"Yeah."

Dale licked her lower lip before she leaned closer. "Maybe we need to look closer to home."

Small puffs of breath tickled Mai's lips. A knock rattled the door and made them both jump as the knob twisted back and forth. "Mai?"

"Out in a minute," Mai yelled and turned on the faucet full. The sound of the water splashing echoed in the tiled space.

"I paid the bill. We can go anytime, Mai," the woman shouted through the door.

Dale pressed her lips together. "Looks like you're going to have to face her down."

Mai squared her shoulders. "Looks like." She shut the water off and stepped around Dale. After smoothing her hands down the front of her pants, she opened the door and stepped out into the foyer of the restaurant. Dale snaked an arm around her waist, her breasts pressing against Mai's arm. Stunned, she froze. The excuse she had worked up in the bathroom dried up in her mouth.

"Darling, why don't you introduce me to your friend?" Dale rested her other hand on Mai's shoulder.

Mai's date, Carol, leaned back and blinked. She narrowed her eyes at Mai. "What is this? Your profile said you were single. I'm no one's side piece. Or into three-ways."

Mai opened her mouth to speak and failed to stifle a squeak as Dale tugged her closer.

"Nope. Not single. And you're not our type. Sorry." Dale's bitchy tone and the heat from Dale's body as she pressed against Mai started a flame low in Mai's belly.

Carol pursed her lips and inclined her head toward Mai. "Un huh. If I were you, I'd keep her chained up, and you might want to check her phone." She glared at Mai. "I can't stand liars."

Carol flounced past them, shoulder checking Mai as she left. Dale stepped away from Mai and smoothed her hand down the front of her dress.

Mai stared at the toes of her shoes. "I deserved that."

"No."

Dale's sharp tone made Mai look up.

"No one should ever feel like they are obligated to provide sex in exchange for dinner. Even at the one decent restaurant between here and Cleveland."

"Thank you. Do they have Uber here?" She pulled her phone from her pocket.

Dale held up her car keys. "Want a ride?" A frown swept over her face. "Unless you have other plans?"

Mai glanced at Dale as she shoved her phone into her pocket. "Nope, no other plans. Not now. And yes, I'd love a ride."

The air was warm after the heavy air-conditioning of the restaurant, and Mai followed Dale to her truck. Their footsteps were loud in the silence between them.

Dale clicked the lock to open the truck. "Would you like to drive?" She dangled the keys from her fingers.

Mai took the keys from Dale's hand. "Yes."

"Marvelous."

Mai opened the passenger door and held out her hand to assist Dale into the truck. She marveled at her sublime body, unable to look away as her dress pulled tight across her ass as Dale mounted the running board and climbed into the pickup truck.

After closing Dale's door, Mai walked around to the driver's side and entered the truck. With a push of a few buttons, she adjusted the rearview and side mirrors and moved the seat forward before she turned to Dale. The glow of the streetlight backlit her profile and full mouth as Dale reapplied her pale-pink lipstick. It took every bit of Mai's willpower not to pull her into a kiss.

Chapter Fourteen

Mai eased the truck onto the blacktop. The road glittered under the moonlight.

"You need to watch for deer." Dale shifted in her seat and the hem of her dress pulled up, exposing her thighs as she slipped off her pumps.

The moon rode the edge of the trees that crowded the road and Mai stole glances at Dale. She had tucked one leg under her, and the hem of her dress was tight over her legs and exposed the top edge of her thigh highs. The rough sound of the rumble strip alerted Mai, and she focused her attention on the road.

"Am I distracting you?" Dale's honeyed tones raised the hairs on Mai's arms.

"Yes."

Dale's rested her palm on Mai's knee before she leaned closer and she traced her fingertips over the back of Mai's neck, making her shiver. "Sorry. Do you want me to stop?"

Mai swallowed hard. "No. Yes. Maybe not while I'm driving."

Dale drew her hand away from Mai's neck. "Take the next left."

Mai glanced at Dale. "This is the way to the lake, isn't it?"

"It is." She stripped off her thigh highs and tucked them into her pumps.

Dale leaned back in the seat and slid her hand over Mai's thigh, the heat from her palm searing. A trickle of desire wet Mai's briefs and she gripped the wheel tighter. She slowed the truck and made the turn onto the dirt road leading to the lake. Popular in her time in high school with those inclined to party and make out, the rough condition of the road and the high weeds growing between the wheel tracks were shaggy evidence of the spot's decline in popularity.

Mai drove slowly, dodging the deeper ruts in the two-wheel track. A dense wood ran alongside the road. Tall trees blocked the moonlight and she switched the headlights to high beam. The trees thinned and a wide grass field ended in a lake. A weathered dock jutted out into the dark water.

Moonlight reflected off the water and lit the field. Mai parked the truck on the grass and pulled the keys from the ignition. The snick of her seat belt as it unfastened echoed in the truck. Dale's palm cupped the back of Mai's neck and she brushed her thumb over the short hairs there.

Mai turned in her seat to face Dale. One hand on the top of the wheel, she leaned in and brushed her lips over hers before she pulled back to look into her eyes. "You sure?"

"Very." Dale tugged Mai close and kissed her as her fingers tightened on Mai's neck. She sighed into Mai's mouth. The soft sound washed over Mai and swept away her doubts.

Mai wrapped her arms around Dale and deepened their kiss as she drowned in the welcoming wet heat of Dale's mouth. Teasing touches of her fingers as she stroked the back of Mai's neck made her tremble.

Mai pulled back to look into Dale's eyes. "This console is digging into my ribs." She drew back and reached under her seat and moved the seat as far as it would go. "Come over here." Mai patted her thighs.

Dale arched her eyebrow. "Nope." She reached behind the seat and pulled a print blanket from the back seat. After tossing the blanket to Mai, she exited the truck.

Mai scrambled to sit up and wrestled with the blanket before she managed to open her door.

Dale stood with her hands on her hips. She inclined her head toward the dock. "This way."

Mai trotted to catch up with Dale's long strides. Her dress wafted about her legs. The delicate scent of Dale's perfume carried on the light breeze and drew Mai toward the promise of more.

*

The dock creaked when Dale stepped on it. The rough wood was warm under her bare feet, cooler in spots as the heat from the sun faded. Mai's footsteps behind her made her turn. Dale gestured toward the end of the dock and Mai fell into step beside her.

The touch of Mai's fingers as she brushed the back of Dale's hand sent a rill of desire through her, and her body turned to flame. At the end of the dock, Mai spread the blanket out. Dale held Mai's eyes as she gripped the hem of her dress and stripped off. She folded it and placed it to the side of the blanket. Mai's gaze was a searing touch as it traveled over Dale's body and lingered on her red lace panties and matching sheer bra. With deliberate motions, Dale lay down on the blanket.

The bluster and high from her drink that had fueled Dale's boldness in the restaurant faded as the moonlight lit her body. Reality pressed down on her, thick and heavy. She covered her soft belly with both hands to hide the myriad of silvery stretch marks and the long white scar that extended from her navel to the top of her pubic bone, a souvenir from the emergency cesarean section she had with Noah. Doubt burned away her desire and she closed her eyes.

"Don't do that." Mai kneeled next to her and took Dale's hands by the wrists. She brought them to her face and nuzzled her palms. "You're gorgeous." Mai bent her head and pressed a kiss to her navel and then trailed a line of kisses over Dale's body. "Absolutely gorgeous."

Mai's words and her kisses settled over Dale and she relaxed into her gentle touches. Her body responded to Mai's reassurances and kisses. She lifted her hands to Mai's shoulders and tugged her into a kiss. Mai's languid attention fanned the flames of want in Dale's body and soul. This. Someone who found her enough. As she was. No masks. No games. Want, raw and unfettered, surged through Dale.

Mai's kisses transformed as her tongue teased and dipped into Dale's mouth. She stroked her hands up and down Dale's sides, her touch fleeting. She palmed Dale's breast and groaned as she thumbed Dale's nipple through the fabric.

Breaking their kiss, Mai kneeled up and stripped her shirt and jog bra off and lay over Dale. Mai's nipples brushed over Dale's belly as she moved over her. The warm length of her body pressed against Dale, her nipples stiff against Dale's skin. Dale lifted her chin to give Mai access to her neck. She trembled under the brush of her lips.

The tight muscles of Mai's ass bunched and flexed under Dale's hands as she held tight and ground against her. Mai kissed her way along Dale's jaw before she moved back to her mouth and possessed her, her kisses setting Dale ablaze.

Her nipples were hard against the lace of her bra and Dale pulled at Mai's belt buckle. "Take your pants off. Now."

Mai stood over her. After toeing off her wingtips, she tugged off her socks and tucked them into her shoes. The moon behind her shaded her face as she unbuckled her belt. The sharp clink of the buckle as it opened echoed off the lake. Mai stripped off her pants.

Dale trailed her fingers over the curve of her calf as Mai folded her pants and placed them next to Dale's dress. "Come here, handsome."

Mai kneeled between her legs before she bent and licked a line along her thigh and pressed her mouth to the wet triangle of fabric between Dale's legs. She mouthed Dale's hard clit through the thin fabric.

Dale gasped. "No."

Mai stopped and raised her head and met Dale's gaze.

"Not yet." Dale reached down, fisted her hand in Mai's hair, and tugged Mai to her.

Wrapping her arms around Mai, she rolled them over. She rose to her knees and unhooked her bra. Leaning forward, she shimmied her breasts free. Mai slid her hands up and under the straps and slipped the bra off Dale's arms. With both hands Mai cupped and squeezed Dale's breasts as she rubbed her thumbs over her stiff nipples. Dale arched into her touch.

Mai hummed. "Your breasts are the stuff dreams are made of." She leaned up and caught a nipple in her mouth.

Dale's laugh turned into a groan as Mai drew her nipple deep and sucked hard. Dale panted when Mai's teeth grazed her skin. "Your dreams?"

Mai answered by flicking her tongue over Dale's nipple again, sending a sharp wave of want through Dale. Fingers tightened over her other nipple as Mai rolled and tugged in a rhythm as her tongue circled Dale's nipple.

Her panties were drenched. She rocked her hips against Mai's tight, hard stomach.

The sensation of being exposed, the chance of being caught, and Mai's unrelenting attentions to her breast detonated Dale's orgasm. She dug her fingers into Mai's silky hair and held her head in place as she rode out her pleasure. A satisfied hum from Mai vibrated against her nipple and a series of aftershocks rippled through Dale.

*

Mai savored the soft fullness of Dale's breasts and the sharp pull on her hair as Dale came. She stroked her thick thighs as she rode out her pleasure. Dale relaxed her grip on Mai's hair. With languorous touches she traced Mai's face as she stared down into her eyes. She leaned forward and Mai released her nipple and nuzzled her neck. Dale hugged her tightly before she shifted to her side and stretched out.

She leaned on her elbow and pinned Mai in place with her thigh as she kissed her way along Mai's neck. "Put your hands over your head."

Mai lifted her hands and knotted her fingers together.

Dale's fingertips traced tight circles over Mai's nipple and then down her belly.

Dale covered Mai's hands with her own, holding her in place as she took her time exploring her body with her other hand. Mai panted as Dale cupped her, fingers rubbing against her fabric-shrouded labia. Top to bottom she stroked, setting a rhythm that had the heel of her hand rubbing against Mai's clit and made Mai desperate for more.

Dale's weight held her in place. The sensation of being captured and held, the hint of being helpless as Dale pleasured her had Mai groaning as she struggled for more of Dale's touch. "Please. Don't stop. It's so good. Don't stop." Mai turned her face and kissed Dale's shoulder and her neck, anywhere her mouth could reach.

Dale slid her hand up and down. Her fingers worked Mai's clit through the wet fabric as she restrained her with her body. She shifted her hand and her fingers tapped over Mai's clit in a steady tattoo. The alternating sensations sent a river of desire flooding through Mai and she soaked her briefs. Dale leaned over her and kissed her, her tongue mimicking her touch. Mai cried out as Dale brought Mai off and a wave of pleasure shot through her.

Dale swallowed her groans as her fingers kept up a constant patter against Mai's now sensitive clit. Mai yipped as Dale switched her tactics and rubbed hard against her. Mai's body shook as she came again, and she cried out as the exquisite sensations rippled through her body. Dale groaned and shifted so she lay over Mai. She aligned their bodies and began a slow grind that had Mai gasping.

The moon lit Dale's pale skin and her breasts swayed as she rocked against Mai. The determined set of her jaw and her purposeful movements had Mai hanging on by a string. Desperate to have Dale come over her, she clutched Dale's shoulders and rocked beneath her, meeting her thrusts. Dale's body juddered and her head fell back on her shoulders as she came with a shout. Mai's orgasm followed, spurred by Dale's thrusts. Dale covered Mai's mouth with her own and kissed her before rolling to her side.

They lay together panting. A breeze blew over them and Dale shivered against Mai's side. Mai wrapped her arm around Dale and flipped the edge of the blanket over them. The weight of what they had done settled over Mai and she swallowed hard. She'd crossed a line. They both had. Their breathing slowed to normal.

Dale rested her hand in the middle of Mai's chest. "Regrets?"

"None at all." Mai kissed the top of Dale's head. "Other than I wish we were in a bed and didn't have to drive home."

Dale pushed up on one arm. She reached for her bra and put it on. "Come on. I know where there's a great bed. They serve a pretty good breakfast too."

"Pretty good?" Mai's feigned distress had Dale giggling. Mai pulled her pants on, stuffed her bra in her pocket, and drew her shirt on. Dale stood up, stretched, and pulled her dress over her head. Mai folded the blanket and tucked it under her arm only to drop it when Dale drew her into a kiss and didn't stop until Mai was gasping.

Chapter Fifteen

The headlights from the truck lit up the driveway and Mai pulled the truck close to the garage door. Dale leaned over and kissed her cheek. "We need to be quiet. Thomas texted. Noah's spending the night at Chip's but Seth's here."

Mai turned her head and kissed her. Her mouth was hot and wet. Dale wrapped her hand in her shirt and held her in place as she kissed her.

Mai's fingers dug into her shoulder, and she broke their kiss. "Can we go inside? I can't do what I want to do to you in this truck."

"How quiet can you be?" Dale licked a line to Mai's ear and then kissed the delicate shell.

"Very."

"Good." Dale slipped away from Mai's arms. She popped the door open, exited, and then closed the truck door gently, bumping it with her hip to make sure it was latched. Mai closed her door and met Dale in front of the truck. She placed her hand in the small of Dale's back as they walked the brick walk around to the side door.

Dale savored the sensation of Mai's touch. The house was dark. Mai unlocked the door and held it open for Dale. With Mai's arm steadying her, she slipped off her pumps and looped their straps over her fingers and crept inside. Mai closed the door behind her and flipped the deadbolt knob. Dale clutched Mai's hand and led her to her bedroom. At the door, Mai stopped without warning. Dale lost her balance and fell against her.

"What?" Dale whispered.

"Are you sure?" Mai's brow was furrowed. "What if he hears us?"

Dale cupped Mai's face and nibbled her way to her ear before she whispered. "I'm the mom. And what if he does? It's my house." She kissed Mai gently. "If you make too much noise, I'll use my panties as a gag. Does that work for you?"

Mai trembled and a tight groan rumbled from her chest. "Oh yes."

Dale pushed the door open and drew Mai inside. She turned and shoved a slide lock in place.

Mai raised her eyebrows. "Lock on the inside?"

"The only way to fly when you have kids who forget to knock when the door is closed."

Dale inclined her head toward the bathroom. "Want to shower with me?" She lifted the hem of her dress and pulled it free of her body.

Mai's gaze settled on her. "Yes." Mai unbuttoned her shirt and tossed it on her dresser. She stepped close to Dale and wrapped her arms around her and drew her into a kiss.

"Let me." Mai opened the clasp of Dale's bra and lifted it from her shoulders, the touch of her fingertips leaving a trail of heat as she removed Dale's bra.

Dale let her head fall back on to her shoulder and closed her eyes. Mai took a nipple in her mouth and sucked gently before she scraped her teeth over the tip.

Her hands settled on Dale's waist and she rubbed her thumbs over Dale's hipbones. She released Dale's nipple and sank to the floor. On her knees, she hooked the edge of Dale's underwear with her fingers and drew them down her legs. Dale rested her hand on the top of Mai's head and lifted each foot in turn as Mai undressed her.

Mai pressed a kiss to the trimmed curls over Dale's clit. "You want me? Want this?"

Dale widened her stance. "Yes. Lick me."

Mai nuzzled her thigh. "Ask nicely." She nipped Dale's thigh.

Dale trembled as Mai gripped her thighs tightly and breathed over her stiff clit.

Dale yanked her hair hard. "Lick me now. I want to come in your mouth."

Mai groaned at the sharp tug on her scalp. Thrilled with Dale's commanding tone, she licked a long line from Dale's swollen labia to her clit. She swirled her tongue over her in fast, hard circles.

Dale covered her mouth with one hand to muffle her cries and gripped Mai's shoulder as she shuddered through her orgasm.

Moonlight filtered through the window and lit Mai's features as she kneeled. She looked up at Dale, her face gleaming, and Dale bent to kiss her. She savored the taste of herself on her lover's lips. Mai stood and shucked off the rest of her clothes.

Dale panted and rested her hand on her chest. "Do you always eat so fast?"

A crooked grin twisted Mai's mouth. "Only when I'm starving." She lifted Dale's hand and kissed the palm. "Still want to shower?"

Dale nodded and let Mai lead her into the bathroom. Mai turned the shower on. "I'll give you a minute." She closed the door, giving Dale privacy while she emptied her bladder. She rolled back the frosted shower door and stepped into the warm spay.

The door opened and Mai joined Dale. Dale wrapped her arms around her. Water flowed over, around, and between them. Dale rubbed her hand over the bar of sandalwood soap and rubbed her hands in slow strokes over Mai's wide shoulders and back. Mai pressed close. The sensation of her firm curves against Dale's body set her aflame.

She cupped Dale's ass with both hands and squeezed. "You're pretty bossy, you know."

"I've been told."

Dale rinsed the soap from her hands. Water ran in her eyes as she leaned in and kissed and nibbled Mai's collarbone. With both hands, she pressed Mai up against the shower tile and pressed her hand between her legs. She used her weight to pin her against the wall.

Mai groaned when Dale teased a finger over her clit. "You're so slick." She pushed inside and Mai's hips lifted. "So eager." Dale stroked in and out. "But for what I want to do to you, we need more room."

Mai reached around Dale and shut the taps off.

Dale smirked and eased back. She flicked Mai's thick brown nipple before she lowered her head and took a long suck.

Mai gasped. "I need to lay down."

Dale stepped away and rolled the shower door open. After passing a towel to Mai, she picked up her own and dried herself, unable to look away from the tantalizing shimmy of Mai's breasts as she dried off.

Dale finished drying herself and hung up her towel. She crooked her finger at Mai and left the bathroom with a saucy swing of her hips.

*

Dale yanked the covers down on the bed. "Make yourself comfortable."

Mai slid onto the worn cotton sheets. She lay back and pillowed her head on her hands.

Dale moved to the dresser. The bright smell of sulfur filled the room and the flare of a match lit Dale's features. She cupped the flame and lit a candle on the dresser. The light scent of lavender bloomed as the wax warmed. The flicker of the flame painted shadows on the bedroom wall.

Mai licked her lips, already missing the taste of Dale that had washed away in the shower. Dale's lips brushed her instep and then her thigh. Her warm breath washed over Mai's clit as she nuzzled her wet curls.

"You smell good." Dale thrust her tongue deep and Mai writhed with pleasure. "And taste divine."

Dale closed her lips around Mai's clit and sucked gently. "And what a lovely fat clit you have." She swiped her tongue over Mai and teased the skin back from the tip with her tongue. "You want me to suck you, baby?"

Dale's voice, low and wanton, flowed over Mai and her clit ached with need.

Dale leaned on her arm and slid two fingers in deep, curling them over Mai's sweet spot. "Or do you want me to fuck you?"

Mai trembled and her nipples peaked. "Do I have to choose?"

Dale stroked deeper and Mai cried out. "No. But you do have to be quiet."

She eased her hand free and left the bed. She returned with a bright-red bandana. "This should help. Do you like to play like this?"

Mai eyed the strip of red cloth and mock pouted. "You said you'd use your panties."

Dale lifted her chin. "Nice answer. Next time. You'll just have to dream about it. Open."

Next time. They would be doing this again. Hope, wild and unfettered, trampled Mai's caution. She opened her mouth and Dale applied the bandana. "If you need me to stop tap my shoulder. Understand?"

Mai nodded her understanding.

Dale kneeled over her, backlit by the candle. "Hands on the headboard."

Mai slipped her hands under the bottom rail of the scrolled brass headboard and held tight.

"Do you know how long I've wanted to do this?" Dale thrust two fingers deep and rubbed the spot that made Mai arch her hips and seek more. She whimpered around her gag. Dale pulled back and thrust in again. "How many times I've wanted to bend you over the kitchen table, yank down your pants, and have you? To fuck you until you screamed my name?"

Mai tongued the rough cloth in her mouth, wet now with her saliva. White knuckled, she clung to the headboard and moaned at Dale's rough-voiced confession as images of Dale taking her filled her mind.

Dale bent and took her clit in her mouth. She sucked languidly, letting Mai's clit pop from between her lips each time she sucked, the lascivious sound filling Mai's ears as the sensation rippled through her body.

Her fingers slid in and out as she slow-fucked Mai. Pleasure snaked and curled around her body, filling her; a deep ache built, and she trembled under Dale's touch.

Dale hummed against her and flicked her clit with her tongue as she added another finger. Mai cried out against the gag, her body tense as a bowstring, nerve endings on fire with sensations. Freedom. Freedom to feel and to let someone else take control of her body and pleasure. Mai moaned her need.

Dale lifted her mouth. "Want to come, baby?"

Mai nodded, her eyes wide.

Dale pinned her in place with her eyes. "Give it to me. Come for me, baby." She lowered her head and sucked Mai's clit, bobbing her head with the motion.

Mai gave in and rolled her head from side to side, relishing the freedom of the gag, and floated on waves of bliss as Dale brought her off, not stopping until she had wrung every single bit of pleasure from Mai's body.

Mai sagged back on the bed. Dale smoothed her hands over her body, soothing her. With swift movements Dale untied the gag and drew it from Mai's mouth. She kissed her, swallowing the last of Mai's groans. Mai let go of the headboard and crushed Dale to her.

Dale pressed her forehead to Mai's. "Are you okay?" She ran her thumb over Mai's lower lip.

Mai sucked her thumb into her mouth and Dale groaned.

"More?"

Mai panted. "Can't get enough of you." She rolled them over until Dale was under her. She rubbed her nose over the silky curve of Dale's neck and inhaled the scent of her skin. "Think you're the only one who's been waiting?" She kissed along Dale's jaw and the tender skin under her ear. "Do you know how many times I stroked myself to sleep thinking of you?" She whispered against the shell of Dale's ear. "How many times I wanted to drop to my knees? To have you command me to lick you until you came in my mouth?"

Dale gripped Mai's hair and tugged her to her mouth and a bruising kiss. Gasping for air, Mai broke their kiss.

Dark fires played in Dale's eyes and made Mai catch her breath. "Do you think you're the only one who likes to be bound?" Dale's eyes were bright, her pupils wide.

"Oh, it's like that, is it?"

Dale panted. "Yes."

Mai kneeled and picked up the bandana. She gathered it in her hands. Dale held her gaze, her lower lip quivering as Mai drew her hands together and bound them with the damp cloth. She left the bed and drew her belt from her pants. Dale's soft groan at the sound made Mai's pulse race.

Once she had bound her hands, Mai stood by the bed and savored the vision of Dale's body, with her legs splayed, hands tied, nipples stiff. She bent, sucked her nipple, and bit lightly. Dale squirmed and Mai drew the belt over her skin, enjoying the way she arched into her mouth.

"Tie me to the headboard."

With one hand she lifted Dale's bound hands over her head and used the belt to secure them to the brass rail.

Mai inhaled sharply, heady from Dale's request. She passed the flat of her hand over Dale's body. "Safe word? Or colors? Red to stop, yellow to slow down? Unless you need me to gag you too?"

The corners of Dale's mouth lifted in a tight smile. "Salt. And I've learned to be quiet."

A flare of jealousy clouded Mai's thoughts as she pondered who might have had the pleasure of teaching Dale to be quiet.

"No." Dale's voice cut into her dark thoughts. "Neither of us come to this innocent or virgins. Don't dwell on what's past. We're here now."

Mai leaned down and kissed Dale, a slow deep kiss, and the tension left her. Now. They had now. She trailed a finger down over the plump curve of Dale's breast. "So, what do you like? Besides being tied up."

Dale lifted her chin and inclined her head toward her chest of drawers. "Look in the top drawer of the dresser."

Mai left the bed. She pulled open the drawer.

"The box on the left."

Mai lifted an intricately carved teak wood box from its place. With one hand she opened the lid. White candles and a lighter were nestled together. "Low melt?"

"Of course." Dale grimaced. "You only make that mistake once."

Mai frowned and pushed away the unreasonable jealousy bubbling in her chest. She brought the box back to the bed. Dale's nipples were peaked, her breath uneven, her legs restless.

Mai placed the box on the nightstand. She drew the backs of her fingers over Dale's belly and then circled her breasts, avoiding her nipples.

Dale panted as Mai ghosted her hands over her skin. "Do it. Now."

Mai straightened. "Patience." She picked up a candle and flicked the lighter to light it. The candle wick flamed to life. Mai held the candle up and let a drop of wax fall on Dale's belly.

Dale closed her eyes and squeezed her legs together. "More," she rasped.

"Open your legs."

Dale spread her legs wide. Mai waited a beat, to savor Dale's trust. With the candle held at an angle, she dripped a line of wax down the center of the deep valley between Dale's breasts. She hissed and arched her back with her lips pressed together to stifle her moan.

"You love this." Mai dripped a line of molten wax down the inside of each of Dale's thighs. She quivered and groaned softly and yanked at her bonds. Her chest rose and fell rapidly, cracking the hardened wax on her chest.

"So much." Dale's quiet ragged voice sent a wave of desire straight to Mai's clit.

Mai grazed the back of her hand over Dale's clit and her hips rocked up, seeking more. She held the candle high and let a fat drop of wax fall onto one of Dale's nipples.

Teeth bared, Dale growled and arched her back, digging her heels into the mattress and pushing her breasts toward Mai. Mai dropped a matching drop of wax on Dale's other nipple.

Dale twisted in her bonds and panted. "Fuck me. Now. Don't make me wait."

Mai snuffed out the candle with her fingers and set it aside. "Topping from the bottom? Why am I not surprised?" Using the edge of her nail, Mai flicked at the white wax with a finger and lifted a bit. The skin was pink underneath.

Dale's eyes were closed, the muscles in her arms taut. Mai drew her fingers over the hard curve of Dale's bicep and then down along the swell of her breast. The bedsprings creaked as Dale rocked her hips and pressed her legs together.

Her body trembled under her touch. Mai flicked the bit of wax over Dale's nipples and a sharp hiss split the air. With both hands Mai pressed Dale's breasts together before she bent her head and licked the tip of Dale's nipple. She sucked first one and then the other nipple into her mouth and laved them alternately with her tongue.

A guttural moan rattled Dale's chest. "Oh, fuck. I'm going to come. Fuck me, I want you inside me when I come. Please."

Mai whispered against her ear. "Finally, the magic word." She stretched out over Dale and cupped Dale's wet heat, sliding her fingers over her clit. Dale jutted her hips up and Mai thrust three fingers deep.

Dale locked her legs around Mai's hips and her lips pulled into a snarl. "Fuck me."

The rough edge of Dale's voice laced with desperation made Mai tremble. Desire. Desire to possess Dale rose, thick and needy, and Mai rolled her body into her thrusts as want dripped down her thighs. "Let go, I got you."

Dale clamped her thighs tightly around Mai's hips, and thrashed wildly. Her mouth open in a silent scream, she came, her body clutching and squeezing Mai's fingers.

Mai bit down on the smooth curve of Dale's shoulder and kept her pace, driving Dale up again, her body opening and welcoming Mai's thrusts.

"Enough," Dale whispered as her body sagged and relaxed under Mai.

Mai eased her fingers from Dale. Using her fingers, slick from Dale's climax, she opened herself and aligned their clits. She closed her eyes against the pleasure and the magical slide of clit on clit as Dale slowly rocked to meet her thrusts. She braced herself on her forearms, caging Dale, and ground against her.

Dale bit her shoulder, her teeth latching tight to the muscle, just short of breaking the skin. She sped up her motions, her body a wild thing under Mai. Electric currents of pleasure whipped through Mai's body and she pressed her face into the pillow to muffle her shout as she came.

Chapter Sixteen

Sunlight outlined the edge of the curtains when Dale woke. Mai's arm was draped over her waist and her body curled around Dale, the big spoon to Dale's little spoon. A pleasant ache between her legs, a souvenir of their night together, made her shift back to feel Mai's soft curls against her ass.

Not wanting to leave the comfort of Mai's body but unable to ignore her bladder's incessant nagging any longer, she lifted Mai's arm and exited the bed. Tiny bits of wax clung to her skin and flaked off as she hustled to the bathroom. She grimaced, already plotting how to get the sheets to the washer without leaving a waxy trail, hard evidence of her kink.

After she relived herself, she brushed her teeth. The beginnings of a bruise showed on her thigh, and she inhaled sharply as her body responded to the memory of Mai's mouth on her skin and between her thighs. *Lucky Yvonne.* Guilt swept over her. And sadness. No future for them other than heartache for Dale. Wrapped in her faded blue terry cloth robe she walked back to the bed.

Mai was awake, a neutral expression on her face. Her jet-black hair stuck up at odd angles.

Dale ached to climb back into bed and rake her fingers through her adorable bed head.

Mai reclined against the pillows with the sheet pulled tightly across her breasts. "Hey." Mai scrubbed a hand over her face.

The easy time they'd had the night before had evaporated with the daylight. Tension swirled between them, the reality of the line they had crossed choking off Dale's words. She grieved their fledgling relationship as if it had been years. Because for Dale it had been years since she had been so smitten. Even with Molly she had held back. Mai was different, so very different. And so very unavailable.

Mai's reticence and lack of enthusiasm grated on Dale. She flushed and raised her hand in acknowledgment of Mai's greeting. "Morning." She swept her hair back with her hand. "About last night..." Dale didn't know what to say that would not open a wider chasm between them. She shifted her gaze to the wall over Mai's head, avoiding her eyes.

Mai slid out from under the covers and bent to gather her clothes. "It's cool. I'll slip out before Seth wakes up." She kept her back to Dale as she dressed. The chill between them swept over Dale and she clutched the robe tighter around her.

"I'm sorry, Mai. I shouldn't have kissed you. I don't... I mean I do—but not with people who are—I'm sorry."

Mai straightened. "What? People who are what?" Her lips curled in a snarl.

"Keep your voice down. You'll wake Seth." Dale hugged her arms around herself and shivered. "People who aren't single. Remember Yvonne? You talk about her all the time. You're even building an apartment to be everything she needs."

"What the hell has my sister got to do with us?" Mai yanked her shirt on, and a button flew across the room and pinged against the wall. "Fuck." She tilted her head back and looked at the ceiling.

"Your sister?" Dale shook her head, sure she had heard incorrectly. "Yvonne is your sister?"

"Yvonne's two years younger than me. Ida went to school with her. She graduated with Yvonne."

Dale rested her hand on her hip. "I was married with two babies by the time my sister graduated. Forgive me if I didn't memorize the graduation roster."

Mai studied Dale from under her furrowed brows. "You thought I was cheating on a partner? That fits if you were looking for something casual." She pursed her lips and exhaled loudly. "Can't say I like it you thought I was a cheater. I may be a lot of things, Dale Miller, but I have never been unfaithful to anyone I was committed to."

Dale pressed her lips together. "I'm not in the market for a relationship. And I've not had the best track record."

Mai buttoned her shirt. "Whatever. Don't stress. We both wanted what happened to happen. You got what you wanted. So did I." She planted her hands on her hips. "Where do we go from here?"

Dale perched on the end of the bed. "I don't know."

Mai snatched her shoes off the floor and hooked them over her finger. She lifted her chin and skewered Dale with her glare. "Well, you know where to find me when you figure it out." The snick of the lock settling into place echoed in the harsh silence between them.

Dale flopped back on the bed and covered her face with both hands. *Not attached. Single. Oh fuck. Single. And a client. Fuck me.*

*

Water splashed against the metal of the electric kettle as Mai filled the pot. She flipped the switch to turn it on. After adding coffee grounds to the French press, she leaned against the kitchen counter as she waited for the water to heat. Her phone vibrated in her pocket. When she thumbed it on, Yvonne's name flashed across the screen and Mai tapped ignore before she stuffed the phone back in her pocket. She looked down the hall toward Dale's bedroom door. *What was I thinking? Her profile makes it clear she's not interested in long term. And thinking I was a cheater. Like it would make a difference? All she wants is sex—what does she care? Unless she does?*

Mai rubbed the back of her neck. The pot clicked off and she poured the boiling water over the coffee grounds. After setting the timer, she took two mugs from the cabinet. The glowering unicorn flashing a rude gesture mug, the one she usually filled for Dale, mocked her and she replaced it. She rubbed her chest and the ache that had settled there.

The timer sounded. She pressed the strainer down and then poured herself a cup of coffee. The hinges on the front door squeaked when she opened it. Sunshine peeked over the hedge and lit one end of the porch. Mai sat in the sunbeam, ready to chase away the chill of an awkward morning after.

The high hedge grew on three sides of the porch, screening it off from the other houses. On Sunday morning it was a private oasis. Even the birds were subdued. Placing her feet on the top rail, Mai tilted back in her chair and called her sister.

Yvonne answered on the second ring. "What's up?"

Mai frowned. "You called me."

Yvonne laughed. "I did but usually when you blow off my Sunday calls you are entertaining. Who is the lucky lady and why aren't you still in bed?"

Mai sighed. "Dale. And it was a one-time thing."

"Dale as in the contractor Dale?" Yvonne sucked in a breath. "Ida's older sister Dale?"

"Yep." Mai sipped her coffee. "And before you start, I know it was a bad idea."

Yvonne snorted. "Isn't she straight? Divorced, has kids?"

"Not so straight. I don't know how she identifies. She was on that stupid app you talked me into using."

"Hold up. You met her through Hit Me Up? I thought you quit that?"

"Nah. Well. For a bit. And we didn't meet that way. I was trying to ditch my snooze fest of a date and Dale acted like we were together."

"She must be some actress. How the hell did you end up in bed?"

"Long story, and I don't kiss and tell." Mai gulped another mouthful of her coffee, savoring the mellow tones of the light roast.

"What are you going to do?"

"As far as I can tell she wants to pretend like it never happened. Her profile said she wanted casual."

"*Jiějie*, you like her. I hear it in your voice. And acting like something never happened is not casual, it's fucked up."

Mai placed her empty coffee cup on the porch rail. "I know. She thought you were my girlfriend. Thought I was cheating on you."

"She thought that? Oh hell, when I get there, I'm going to poke her with my cane."

"We cleared it up. But now"—Mai wiped her sweaty palm on her jeans—"I don't know what to do."

"You need me to come there and kick her ass?"

Mai laughed. "Nah. She's not bad. Just afraid. She's been with some real winners. The last one took her for a bundle. She almost lost her business."

"Be careful. I hear love in your voice."

Mai rubbed the back of her neck, trying to soothe the stubborn tightness there. "I'm not in love."

"Yet. And don't fall in love. She'll break your heart."

Too late. "I won't. So why did you call me?"

"The settlement came through."

"For real?"

"Yep. Don't worry about the renovation costs. Or really any costs going forward. We're loaded."

Mai blinked. *I don't have a reason to crash here. Or teach Noah.*

"You there?"

"I can't believe it."

"Me either but it's true. We should have the first payment next week. I'm going to buy my ticket. What airport is closer—Columbus or Cleveland?"

"It's almost equal. Find the best deal."

Yvonne snorted. "When you say that all I can hear is Mom's voice."

"That's good business." Mai mimicked her mother's favorite phrase in her lilting accent.

"I'm hanging up. I'll text you my itinerary. Love you."

"Love you." Mai thumbed off the phone. She snagged her coffee cup and tilted it up, catching the last few bitter drops on her tongue. The crispness of the morning settled in her bones. Bread. A good day to make some bread. Kneading dough was the perfect meditative activity when she wanted to puzzle out anything. And today Dale Miller was the enigma she wanted to sort out.

Mai turned her empty cup in her hands and studied the pattern of branches on the evergreen unseeing, her mind filled with images of Dale and their night together. The way Dale had stepped up and pretended to be with Mai, and then the dock. Mai had been shocked by her willingness to get naked on the dock but the convenience of the blanket in the back of the truck seemed like not a coincidence. *What if the woman she had a date with had been more to her taste? Was I just a willing substitute? Someone to get her off?* Mai huffed out her breath.

Her own date had been a desperate attempt to rid herself of her attraction to Dale. And now. Now it was worse. Now she had a taste and wanted more. And it was not going to happen. Yvonne was right. She was leaning over the edge of falling down the rabbit hole of being in love with Dale. After placing her empty cup on the table, she closed her eyes and slouched down in the chair.

The Sunday smell of laundry detergent wafted on the breeze, reminding Mai she needed to do a load of wash. She chewed the inside of her cheek. *Sexy Sunday. Laundry. Bread baking. Reading. Anything to keep my mind off her. Who would have thought she was such a wild thing? Maybe I should look for a room to rent. Some distance might be a good thing. I could set up a more formal thing with Noah.*

A twinge of sorrow tweaked her heart. Noah was the kid she'd never known she wanted. Not her kid, not even close, but the closest thing she was going to have in this lifetime. Mai braced her arms on her knees and rested her chin in her hands. *Not going to fix it sitting here feeling sorry for myself.*

*

Mai startled with the squeak of the door hinges. Dale held up the French press. "Thought you might want a refill."

Mai's cautious expression pricked Dale's conscience. "I owe you an apology."

Mai looked down at her hands. "It's fine."

"No, it's not. Look at me"—Dale placed the coffee press on the table—"please."

Mai looked up and Dale cupped the back of her neck and kissed her gently. Mai moaned and opened to her kiss, and she gripped the collar of Dale's robe, holding her in place.

Dale broke their kiss and leaned her brow against Mai's forehead. "I should've known you weren't a cheater. You've been nothing but honest with me. I'm sorry I said what I did."

Mai rested her hand on Dale's arm. "I might have overreacted."

"No. Don't do that. Your feelings are valid, Mai. Don't discount them."

Dale kissed her again, a long slow kiss. Mai's tiny noises of need rocketed through Dale. She carded her fingers through Mai's silky hair before she closed her fingers and gripped a handful. Dale tugged her head back and nuzzled her neck, dropping kisses along her throat. "As nice as it is on the porch this morning, I'd like to take this discussion indoors." She pulled back to search Mai's eyes. "If you want."

Mai held Dale's gaze. "I want." She leaned forward and pulled Dale into a deep kiss. "Lead the way, Ms. Miller."

Dale tugged Mai up from her chair and gathered her into her arms and kissed her. Mai relaxed into her embrace. Dale broke their kiss and trailed kisses along her neck. Mai swept her hands up and cupped Dale's breasts. Dale's body responded, her nipples tightened, rubbed against the rough fabric of the robe. "I need to shower and get the rest of this wax off. Join me?" She spoke against the shell of Mai's ear.

"Depends."

Dale held Mai by her shoulders and peered into her face. "On what? We've a fifty-gallon tank if you're worried about enough hot water."

Mai traced her lower lip with her tongue. "Not worried about the water. I want to set some boundaries. You know, make sure we're both on the same page."

Dale swallowed hard as she remembered the shattering orgasms she'd had with Mai's mouth on her. "I... Yes? What do you want?"

"Will you let me wash your back?" Mai pulled Dale's robe open, stopping short of exposing her nipples. She walked her fingers along the deep valley between her breasts.

"Yes," husked Dale as a surge of wetness coated her bare thighs.

Mai lifted her hand and rubbed the back of her knuckles over Dale's throat. "And do anything else I might want to do to you in the shower?"

Dale shivered at the sensual threat in Mai's voice.

"Let's go." She laced their fingers together and drew Mai along behind her.

*

They crept into the house hand in hand.

Mai glanced up at the door to the basement stairs. "How long do you think we have before he's up?"

Dale pulled her along the hallway. "Not long. Hurry." She pushed the door to her room open and dragged Mai inside. She spun Mai around and pressed her up against the door. Lacing their fingers together, she lifted Mai's arms over her head and pinned them against the door. The backs of her hands pressed against the cool wood while her body burst into flames everywhere Dale's body pressed against her. With a teasing bump, Dale ground against her hips.

Mai shuddered and gasped. "I thought you wanted to shower." Dale ground against her again and Mai shuddered.

Dale trailed a line of kisses along Mai's throat and then nipped the delicate skin under her ear. "Couldn't help myself. I want to be inside you."

She cuffed Mai's hands in one of her own and slid the other down her body. She thumbed open the top button of Mai's pants and shoved past her briefs. And then her fingers were skating over Mai's slick hard clit. Mai spread her legs as far as the pants would let her and angled her hips.

Dale groaned as they slid home, two fingers deep, and rocked into Mai. "I love how hot and wet you are." She curled her fingers and stroked the spot that made Mai's knees weak and her hips rock, seeking more. She braced herself against the door while Dale took her time fucking her.

Her head resting against the curve of Dale's neck, she panted as waves of pleasure spiraled out from her core. Dale shifted the angle of her thrust. The heel of her hand ground against Mai's clit and she spilled over Dale's hand, biting the collar of Dale's robe to keep from crying out.

Dale released her hand and kissed her. Mai drew her close, wrapping both arms around her. "Shower. Now."

"Shower." Dale stepped back and dropped her robe. She turned and looked over her shoulder at Mai, raking her gaze over her body. "Coming?" she called softly as she sauntered into the bathroom.

Mai shucked her clothes off and trotted after her.

The drum of the shower on the tiles was loud in the small space. Dale took two towels from the shelves over the toilet and placed them on the countertop.

"You're glorious." Mai gathered Dale's heavy breasts in her hands and bent her head to lick each nipple in turn.

Dale arched into Mai's mouth and dug her short nails into her shoulders as she clung to her. "Mmm, that's good."

Mai let Dale's nipple pop from her mouth. She pulled the shower door back before she stepped into the bathtub. "This tub is huge."

"Perks of being a contractor. I salvaged it from a remodel I did. The homeowner didn't want it."

Mai moved under the hot spray to give Dale space. The door scraped along the track as Dale pushed it closed, sealing them off.

"Stand here." Mai pointed to the front of the shower. "Turn around." Mai soaped her hands. Water dripped and flowed over the sensuous curves of Dale's body. Mai spread her hands out and swept them over her shoulders. The sandalwood scent of the soap surrounded them, and Mai wrapped her arms around Dale. She held a breast in each hand and Dale's nipples hardened under her touch, pressing into her palms.

Mai bent her knees and rubbed her body up and down Dale's back and ass, the slide of the soap delicious with their full body contact. Dale gasped and braced her hands against the shower tiles. Mai thumbed her nipples and then plucked at them. A deep groan reverberated off the shower walls and Dale tilted her head back.

"Shh." Mai licked a trail along Dale's neck as she ground against her ass. "I thought you said you could be quiet." She rinsed the soap from her hands in the warm spray. She cupped Dale and squeezed. Dale bucked into her hand. Mai spread her fingers, index and ring on either side of Dale's clit and her middle finger brushed over Dale's thick clit. She stroked languidly. Dale body tensed and she moaned. "What are you doing to me? It feels so good. Don't stop. Please, don't stop."

"Never." Mai tweaked Dale's nipple as she jacked her clit.

Dale panted. "I...I...Oh." She clamped her hand over her mouth to muffle her scream as she came. Mai banded an arm around her waist and supported her as she shuddered through her orgasm.

She relaxed, leaned back into Mai's arms, and reached back to cup her face. Mai leaned her cheek against Dale's face and closed her eyes against the spray.

They stayed like that, a moment, and a lifetime, as the water washed away the awkwardness of their morning.

Dale turned and locked her arms around Mai's waist. "Bed? Or do you have other plans for today?"

Desire, heady and rich, swirled in the depths of Dale's eyes. And something else. Something Mai wasn't ready to believe. Affection. Tenderness.

"I didn't have any plans for the day."

Dale reached behind her and shut the shower off. Mai shoved the door back, and steam billowed around them. After grabbing a towel and passing it to Dale, she stepped out to the tub and picked up her towel and dried herself. She leaned in and kissed Dale. "But I think we might need a bit of breakfast first. Aren't you hungry?"

"Yes. But not for food." Dale's half smile made Mai's stomach flutter.

Dale tossed her towel to the floor and kneeled on it. With both hands she yanked Mai's towel aside and threw it on the counter. She slid her hands up the back of Mai's thighs and pulled her close. Her mouth settled over Mai and she licked a slow line from her labia to her clit before she took her in her mouth and sucked. Her lips pursed, her wet hair hung in limp strands, and her breasts swayed as she worked Mai's clit.

Jolts of pleasure shot through her and Mai held tight to Dale's shoulders as she took her hard and fast. She curled over her and came with a stifled cry. Dale swiped her tongue over her clit and Mai shuddered through the aftershocks. Dale rose and wrapped Mai in her towel.

Mai's hands trembled as she cozied herself in her towel. "Breakfast. And then bed."

Chapter Seventeen

Mai whipped the eggs to a creamy pale-yellow.

Dale grated sharp cheddar cheese. "Is this enough?"

Mai glanced at the pile of cheese shreds on the plate. "Perfect. Like you."

Dale placed the grater in the sink. "Not saying that to get laid, are you?"

Mai laughed. "Nah, I don't think it would take that much."

"Pretty cocky now you've got into my panties, aren't you?" Dale wrapped her arms around Mai's waist and nipped the side of her neck.

Mai yipped and slopped a bit of egg down the side of the bowl. "Hey. No fair."

Dale soothed the nip with her mouth. "Hurry up. I have plans for you."

Mai groaned. "You make it hard to cook, ya know." She wiped her hands off and then patted Dale's hands. "Go. Sit. Over there or I'll never get breakfast finished."

Dale stepped back and held up her hands. "Got it."

She sat down across from Mai and studied her as she cooked their omelet. The scent of butter as it melted in the pan filled the kitchen. Mai pushed the button on the toaster and then poured the egg mixture into the hot pan. With sure motions she tilted the pan and the liquid egg spread out and solidified. Minutes later, Dale was taking her first bite of the sublime breakfast Mai had prepared as easy for her as breathing.

The rattle and squeak of the back door opening followed by Noah's appearance in the kitchen brought the harsh realization she and Mai would not be able to continue their sexy plans.

Unless she wanted Noah to know. No, that couldn't happen. Noah would be devastated when Mai left if he thought Dale and Mai were a couple. No forever. Not for them. Just a for now. One night and a long morning after. Her stomach knotted. What the hell was she thinking playing house with someone who had been out looking for the same thing Dale had wanted? A hookup. Sex with no responsibility.

Mai's hand on her thigh made her start and she spilled her juice into her plate, spoiling her breakfast. She launched herself off the bar stool and grabbed a kitchen towel to mop up her juice. "Noah! Hey!" Dale hugged her son and met Mai's gaze over his shoulder, as she tossed her the dish towel, pleading with her eyes for Mai to not acknowledge what had gone on between them.

Mai's expression shuttered.

"I was gone overnight, Mom." Noah wiggled out of Dale's hug. His gaze shifted between Dale and Mai.

Mai pursed her lips as she finished mopping up the mess, collected their plates, and placed them next to the sink. The splash of water in the drain brought Dale out of her fog.

"Why don't you use the dishwasher?"

Mai frowned at Dale. "What?"

Dale tugged open the door to the dishwasher. "I fixed it. Bad wire. And I replaced the seal." She held out her hand toward Mai. "You scrape, I'll load."

Noah whooped. "All right, Mom! I was sick of washing dishes."

Mai's gaze settled on Dale and heat rose in her face. Dale shifted her gaze to her hands, avoiding her eyes. "Sorry it took me so long to fix it. I should've made it a priority."

Mai's hand brushed hers as she passed her a dish. "Sometimes it takes someone else showing us how much easier our life could be if we fix the stuff we've let slide."

Noah slouched onto a bar stool and snagged an apple from the bowl on the counter. "I've got homework. This summer school stuff is intense." He raised his eyebrows at Mai. "What do I need to do for dinner tonight?" He took a bite of the apple.

"Nothing. I got this. Homework is a priority."

Noah finished his apple while Dale and Mai loaded the dishwasher in silence. Dale's chest squeezed tight. Mai's icy demeanor and stiffness was torture. She longed for the easy time they had and wondered how to get back there.

*

"You find everything?" The grocery clerk scanned their purchases. She batted her eyes at Noah and her heavy blue eye shadow flaked at the corners.

"Yeah, Brandy, we found everything." Noah handed the envelope with their grocery money to Mai.

"You going to Kelly's party Saturday?" Brandy twisted her long hair streaked with purple around her fingers.

"Not sure." He ducked his head and stepped along the counter to help bag their groceries.

Mai bit her lip as she watched the blush creep up Noah's neck.

"Eighty-three dollars and forty-nine cents is your total."

Mai drew two twenties from the envelope and then pulled her money clip from her pocket and peeled off two more twenty-dollar bills and a five. She handed them to her clerk.

The cashier's face scrunched up as she pulled a counterfeit bill checker marker and highlighted each twenty-dollar bill. She cracked her gum and then smiled at Mai. "You visiting or passing through?"

"She's staying with us, for now. She used to live here. Before she had her show."

Brandy tilted her head and studied Mai. "For real?"

Mai sighed. "For real."

Brandy gave Mai her change. "Why'd you come back?" She snorted. "If I get out of here, I'm not coming back. You gonna stay?"

Mai sensed Noah's gaze on her. "I am. For now." She glanced up. Noah's eyes were dark. He settled the last bag in their cart and walked away pushing their cart.

Mai shoved her change in her pocket and hurried after him.

Noah's hunched shoulders and his stiff posture as he loaded the cab of the truck with the groceries made Mai huff out a breath.

She waited until they were on their way back to Noah's house to speak. "I'm planning on staying, Noah. But if Yvonne needs to live closer to a large medical center, I'm going to move us there."

"Cleveland Clinic is an hour from us. Would she need more than that?"

"I don't know. UCLA has managed to keep her condition stable, but it could change suddenly."

Noah chewed his lip as he kept his gaze on the road. "I get it."

"Do you?" Mai drummed her fingers on her knees. "It's not something I can control, Noah. I left before because I had something to prove to everyone."

"And now?" He flipped the blinker lever on with his hand as he slowed the truck to make a left turn.

"I don't have to prove anything to anyone but myself. I was selfish when I left. I left my mom to deal with the restaurant and my sister." Mai swallowed on a dry throat. "It was too much. My mom had a heart attack a year later."

"That's not your fault."

Mai rolled the hem of her shirt between her fingers. "I would have been there. Yvonne wouldn't have been the one to find her."

"When my grandma passed, my grandpa and I were in the workshop. He and I were making a fancy box for Mom's birthday. We came in for lunch and she was gone. He still thinks it was his fault she died. That if he had been there, he could have called 9-1-1 and she would still be here." Noah's voice broke. "And I blamed myself because I bugged him about making the box because Mom was going through a sad time and I wanted to make her happy." Noah pulled into the driveway and turned the car off. He swiped at his nose with his sleeve. "But the doctor said it wouldn't have made a difference. Grandma had an aneurism. He said even if she'd been in the hospital, she wouldn't have made it."

Mai reached over and squeezed Noah's shoulder. "My head says you're right, but my heart still feels like it wasn't right to leave. I was angry. My mom was ridiculous when

I came out to her. Pretended like she hadn't heard me. Acted like I was invisible unless she needed something. Never acknowledged all the things I did after my father died to keep the restaurant going. When I had the opportunity to leave, I did."

Noah slouched in his seat. Mai shifted her gaze from his face to the baby-blue Electric glide motorcycle parked in front of the house. "Who's here?"

Noah glanced in the sideview mirror. "Sidney." He popped the locks on the truck.

"The security guard from the farmer's market?" Mai's heart squeezed hard. "Thought you said they broke up."

Noah shrugged. "I thought they did. Maybe Mom changed her mind." He pinned Mai in place with his gaze. "Not like she's got any reason not to date her."

Mai shoved aside the vicious wave of jealousy that swept over her. "Yeah."

*

The low murmur of voices from the living room made Mai grit her teeth. Noah kicked the door closed behind them. Mai set her bag on the counter.

"Hey partner, how about not slamming the door?" Sidney's bulky frame filled the doorway to the living room.

Noah ignored her and turned to Mai. "Should I leave the eggs out to get to room temperature?"

"I spoke to you, Noah." Sidney's voice had dropped to a menacing growl.

"You did. And you're not my mom." Noah turned his back to Sidney and busied himself with putting groceries away.

Dale cleared her throat. "Sidney was just leaving."

"I don't have to rush off." Sidney dragged a kitchen chair over and plopped into it. She stretched her legs out and crossed her arms over her chest. "I have time. I haven't met your—friend?"

Mai drew herself up and met Sidney's taunting gaze. "Mai Li."

Sidney crossed her legs at the ankle and a bit of red dirt fell off her boots. "Seen you at the farmer's market. Talking to Sally. Spent a long time at her stall."

Mai washed a bunch of grapes and laid them in a colander to dry. She tucked two pears into the fruit bowl on the counter. "She has lovely produce."

"Well, that's one way to say it." Sidney's leer made Mai want to wipe it off with a skillet. Sidney latched on to Dale's arm and rubbed her thumb over her wrist. "Dale and I used to go to the farmer's market with Noah. Before he got all sassy mouth."

Noah slammed a cabinet shut behind Mai.

Dale yanked her arm away from Sidney's touch and rubbed the back of her hand on her jeans. "Once. We went once. And it's time for you to go."

"We're getting to know each other. What's your business, Mai?"

"My business is my business. Dale has asked you to leave. Twice now." She rested her hands on her hips and glared at Sidney.

Sidney rose from the chair. "I could make it my business."

Mai held her ground and met Sidney's hard look with one of her own.

Sidney's eyes narrowed. "Where're you from anyway?"

Mai pursed her lips. "I don't owe you an explanation of any kind. You have no authority in this house. Or anywhere else unless you're being paid to work as security." She tilted her head toward Dale. "And if my friend is not inclined to press this, I am." Mai walked around the end of the bar as she dried her hands on the dish towel. "Get out. Now. You are not welcome here."

Sidney's face grew red and her jaw bulged where she tightened it. "No one talks to me like that."

Mai widened her stance. "You're a bully. And rude. And bitter."

Dale moved to stand shoulder to shoulder with Mai. Noah moved and stood behind the two of them. "Leave now, Sidney. Don't come back. I've made my position clear. We are over."

"But why?" Sidney's face crumpled in confusion.

"Because I'm not in love with you. I never was. We dated for six months, and then it was over. It's been over since last year. I don't know how else to spell it out for you. I don't want to be with you. Leave. Now."

Sidney shoved the chair back under the table roughly and stormed from the house. The roar of her motorcycle as she started it with its loud pipes rattled the windows. The noise faded she drove off.

Dale rested her hand on Mai's forearm. "Thank you."

Mai chewed her lip. "Has she ever threatened you? Or Noah?" She twisted the kitchen towel in her hands.

"No. She's harmless. More bark than bite."

Mai shrugged. "If you say so." She turned back toward the kitchen.

Dale grabbed her arm and spun her into her arms. She looked into Mai's eyes before she drew her into a deep kiss. "Don't worry about her."

Mai dropped the kitchen towel she was holding and hugged Dale to her. She looked over her shoulder and right into Noah's wide-eyed face.

*

Dale circled to come up on the side of the line for Mai's rolled omelet stall. Winding across the center square, it stretched past the bell stand on the far side of the square. She observed Noah as he took the orders and set up the ingredients. A broad smile on his face even as he hustled to keep up. Mai's back was to Dale as she worked two omelet pans on the two-burner stove at the rear of the stall. She stepped over the sandbags holding the popup awning in place and worked her way to stand in front of the cooktop.

"You take special orders?" Dale pitched her voice low, for Mai's ears alone.

Mai glanced up and into Dale's eyes. "Depends."

"On what?"

Mai tilted the pan and a perfectly browned omelet slid onto the paper plate waiting for it. She sprinkled a bit of fine herbs over the top and passed it to Noah. "On what you want to trade for it." Her eyes gleamed.

Dale's pulse sped up as a flush spread over her face. "I'm sure we can come to some agreement."

Mai turned out another omelet. Noah appeared at her shoulder. "Hey, Mom. Mai, how are we doing on supplies?"

Mai eyed the jug of premixed eggs and the remaining cheese and bacon pieces. "We have enough for about twenty more bacon and cheese omelets. And ten plain after."

Noah turned back to his position at the front.

"He looks happy."

Mai grinned at Dale. "It's like anything else you like to do, it's not work. He's high off the energy of the crowd and the hustle. He's got the makings of a line chef. He's cool, even when it gets super busy. Before you came, we had an order for six omelets from the folks over at the pottery stall."

Dale's phone vibrated. "Sorry, it's Seth." She stepped away from the booth to take the call.

"Hey, are you coming? I need you to see this mess of wiring. I don't want to touch it."

"Be there in five." She thumbed the phone off. When she turned back a steaming omelet on a plate was next to the stove.

Mai inclined her head as she wiped out the omelet pan. "That one's yours."

"What do I owe you?" She picked up her plate, cut the omelet with her fork and took a bite, and chewed slowly while she held Mai's gaze.

Mai looked at Dale from the tops of her eyes. "We can work it out later." Her mouth pulled into a wolfish grin.

Dale finished her omelet in four bites and whispered, "Oh, I'm sure we can. I'm positive I have something you want." She held Mai's gaze long enough to enjoy the dull red blush spreading over her cheeks.

"See you at home, Noah," Dale called. She stepped back and turned toward the parking lot. Sidney's hot glare disturbed her mellow feelings and she made a sharp turn to avoid walking past her, desperate to hold on to the flirty glow that warmed her belly and her heart.

*

Mai snuggled into the soft curve of Dale's breasts and pressed close. The steady thump of Dale's heartbeat in her ear soothed her. Drowsy after their lovemaking, because Mai was lying to herself if she thought it was sex now. It was love. Love, full throttle, bearing down on them both, no matter how Dale tried to pretend otherwise. Mai saw it her eyes and sensed it in every touch. Love. The one thing she was certain she would not find back in her hometown had taken her by surprise.

Dale carded her fingers through Mai's hair. "You awake enough I can ask you a question?"

"Isn't that a question?"

Dale tugged her hair. "You're such a smart-ass sometimes. And yes."

"So, ask." Mai rested her hand on the curve of Dale's stomach.

"My sister Ida is getting married. Again."

Mai rose on her elbow to look Dale in the face. "And? You want me to do the food?"

Dale frowned. "No. I want you to come with me. As my date."

"You want to out us as a couple at your sister's wedding?"

"Half the town thinks we already are. What's the problem?"

Mai sat up and took Dale's hand and laced their fingers together. "No problem on my end. But we've only told Noah."

"If Noah knows, all the boys know." Dale looked away from Mai's face. "Are you afraid to be seen with me? Afraid it will cut into your dating opportunities?"

Mai reached over and cupped her face. "Look at me. Please?"

Dale's eyes were bright.

Mai kissed her. "I'd be more than happy to go with you. I'm not ashamed of you. Why would you ever think that?"

"I'm not exactly your type." She passed her hand over her body.

The insecurity in Dale's gaze undid Mai. "What are you talking about?" She drew her into a deep kiss. "You are everything I've ever wanted. Smart, hardworking. Generous, kind. And sexy as hell."

"Don't. Don't say things you don't mean." Dale pressed her lips together in a firm line.

"I don't blow smoke up anyone's ass. I..." Mai bit back the words she was terrified to say, to admit, even to herself. "I care for you, Dale. I'd like to accompany you to Ida's wedding."

Dale tugged her down and rolled them over. Her eyes were dark. "Thank you." She caged Mai with her arms and kissed her fiercely. "Even if you don't mean any of the sweet things you said it was nice to hear. And thank you."

Mai gripped Dale's hips and held fast. "I meant every word. And someday you're going to believe me the first time I tell you something."

"Someday." Dale settled her head against Mai's shoulder.

Mai twisted a lock of Dale's smooth hair between her fingers. "You're so bold when we are in the middle of a scene. You're a kickass top. And outside this room you run your own business and are hard-ass enough you can push a crew to get jobs finished on time under or on budget. How can you be this insecure about our relationship?"

"Because I have a fucking awful habit of picking the wrong folks. Bill. Molly. That psycho Sidney." Dale burrowed her face into Mai's neck. "I let Molly spend me into near bankruptcy. I'm still digging out of that hole."

"I'm not them." Mai rubbed Dale's back in slow circles and kissed her forehead. "And you didn't pick me. I showed up."

Dale raised her head and held Mai's gaze. "I'm still me. Give me time."

Mai brushed her lips over Dale's mouth. "As much as you need."

Chapter Eighteen

Tea lights lit up the branches of the large maple in her father's yard, and a score of pickups and SUVs crowded the front yard. Dale pulled the truck into a space next to the porch. She turned and handed the keys to Thomas. Thomas pocketed them. "Doesn't mean you can get shit-faced, Mom."

Seth guffawed as he opened the back door. "Good one." Noah and Mai followed Seth as they exited the truck.

Dale pushed open her door. "Language. And that was not my plan." Dale turned a steely gaze on Seth. "Goes for you too. I don't want to have to pour you into the truck. And you know the family rule about drinking and getting sick."

"You bring it up, you clean it up," the boys chorused as one.

Mai stepped around the truck and held her hand out to help Dale down from the truck. "You have them well trained."

Dale took Mai's hand and stepped down to the ground. She slammed her door shut. "I do." She took Mai's arm, curling her fingers around the firm curve of her bicep.

The baby-blue linen shirt and navy-blue suit jacket she wore with fitted trousers had Dale wanting nothing more than to sneak off to a quiet corner to slip her hands under the coat and feel the strong graceful curves of Mai's back. Her wrap fluttered as a gust of wind rattled the stubs of corn stalks left in the field surrounding her father's home. They followed the sounds of the crowd to the rear of the house. An arch wrapped in silk ivy with faux red roses was set up between aisles of white chairs. Dale's father clapped Mai on the back and Dale held tight when Mai flinched.

"I knew it." His beard was plaited into one long braid with a purple ribbon twisted in it. Eyes twinkling, he released Mai and waved his hand toward the right side of the two groups of chairs. "Sit on the bride's side. Unless it looks like Jeff's side is empty then slide over to balance it out."

"Sure, Dad." She led Mai away from her father. "See? That went well."

Mai grimaced. "Your dad was worse than Noah about us getting together." Her brows drew down. "Did you tell your sister you were bringing me?"

"No. But I had marked plus one on my invitation."

Mai pursed her lips. "I'm Sidney's replacement."

Dale lifted her chin. "Nope. Don't do that. You are my date. And Sidney was a stupid mistake. We were over a year ago. I had planned to invite Mrs. Rice."

"Speaking of mistakes." Mai frowned.

Sidney sauntered through the crowd of wedding guests toward them.

Mai leaned close to Dale. "Why is she here?"

Dale shifted and turned her back on the approaching Sidney. "She's Jeff's cousin." She squeezed Mai's hand. "I have to go find my sister. I forgot my clutch in the car and my sister's present is in it. Will you find Thomas and get it for me?"

"Sure."

Dale leaned in and brushed a kiss over Mai's lips.

"I won't be long." Mai walked in the direction Thomas had gone.

Dale stepped up onto the porch.

"Nice to see you, Dale."

Sidney's oily tone made Dale clench her jaw and she rounded on her. "I don't want to talk to you."

"Got some information for you." She looked over her shoulder and lifted her chin toward Mai. "I only have your best interest at heart."

Dale raised an eyebrow. "I doubt that but if I means you will leave me in peace, spill."

"She's been arrested. Spent time in jail. For embezzlement."

"Get away from me. Now. Don't speak to me again. And if you spread that lie to anyone here you will be the sorriest woman on this earth." Dale took a step toward Sidney. "I'll report you for abusing your position."

Sidney's sick smile spread across her face. "It's not abusing my position to check on people who refuse to cooperate."

"You are no longer with the sheriff's department. Get away from me."

"Dale?" Mai stopped two feet behind Sidney. She held up Dale's clutch. "Got it." She shifted her gaze between Dale and Sidney. "Everything all right?"

Sidney spun on her heel and took a quick step toward Mai. "You tell me. Anything you want to tell Dale about your time in Corona?" She planted her hands on her hips.

"What?" Mai raised an eyebrow. "What the hell are you talking about?"

Sidney lifted her chin. "Corona, 2007 ring a bell?"

Mai glared at Sidney. "Yeah, I was there for a bit." She stepped around Sidney and passed the handbag to Dale. "You okay?"

Dale looked to Mai's face. "It's not true, is it?"

"Is what true? Yes. I was there. Something wrong with that?"

Sidney rested her hands on her hips. "I've got my eyes on you. You might fool Dale, but I know trouble when I see it." She turned on her heel and walked away.

Dale pursed her lips.

Mai frowned at Dale. "What did she tell you?"

"That you had spent time in prison in Corona. For embezzlement. Is it true?"

Mai's eyes shuttered. "And you believe her?"

"She has access to records." Dale hung her head. "It wouldn't matter."

Mai backed away from Dale and held up both hands. She opened her mouth as if to speak and then she closed it and jammed her hands into her pants pockets and turned away from Dale.

Dale studied the angry set of her shoulders, unable to parse apart her behavior. She hurried through the screen door and walked to the bedroom she had shared with her sister growing up. Her sister was sitting on one of the twin beds with her face pale and her hands were knotted together in her lap.

"You okay?" Dale sat next to her sister. "Having second thoughts?"

"No. Nerves."

Dale unzipped her purse and pulled out a box covered in worn blue velvet. "Open it."

Ida opened the box with trembling fingers.

A delicate blue enamel forget-me-not on a gold chain lay on the white tissue paper.

"Oh, Dale. This was Mom's." Tears filled her sister's eyes.

"It was. Dad gave it to me when I married Bill." She lifted the necklace. "Turn around and let me put it on you."

Ida twisted away from her and Dale fastened the necklace in place. She turned back to Dale. "Thank you." She hugged her close.

Dale patted her back. "Damn it. I wasn't going to cry until later."

Ida sat back and snagged a tissue off the nightstand. She dabbed at her eyes. "You okay? I know you don't like Jeff."

Dale rubbed her sister's arm. "It doesn't matter what I think. You love him?"

"I do. And he's a good guy, Dale. He had a bad start, that's all." She looked Dale in the eye. "Did you bring the mysterious Mai? Is it serious with you too?"

"I did." Dale pressed her lips together. "And I don't know."

Her sister frowned. "I know that look. What's up?"

"Sidney said something, and I asked Mai about it. And she didn't deny it. Got angry and walked away."

"Why would Sidney lie?"

"Because she's still upset that I broke up with her? Or maybe she is telling the truth, and Mai is lying."

"Sis, you have to take care of you. And Mai should confirm or deny whatever Sidney said."

Dale hugged herself. "I think she was hurt I asked at all, that I even considered Sidney was telling the truth."

"You care about her. A lot. So, ask again. Let her cool off. Would it make a difference in how you feel about her?"

Dale pursed her lips. "Does Jeff having had a rough start make you feel different about him?"

"Nope." Ida picked up Dale's hand. "And if you love her you need to ask again. And make her believe it wouldn't matter."

"Are you ready?" Eli poked his head into the room.

"As I'm going to be." Ida stood up and Dale rose with her.

Her father led them out of the house. The chairs were filled now, and Dale searched the crowd for Mai. She sat at the end of the second row next to Noah. Thomas and Seth sat next to him. A program lay on an empty seat next to Seth. Mai's back was straight, her head high as she perched on the edge of the chair.

The three seats between them seemed like miles as Dale took the seat next to Seth. Jeff and his best man, resplendent in their well-groomed beards and tweed vests, stood to the left of the minster. The wedding march played, and everyone rose to watch Ida proceed down the aisle.

Sidney's smug expression when Dale approached the empty seat next to Seth told her everything she needed to know about Sidney's intentions. Even if it were true, was it something Dale needed to know? Mai had been honest with her, never given Dale a reason to think she was hiding something. And had done so many little things over the last five months to make Dale's life easier. Dale touched her lips remembering Mai's kisses and words as they prepared for the wedding. How she had looked at Dale, her eyes full of mischief and promise.

Dale glanced toward Mai and caught her gaze. Mai's face was stone, her eyes dark, and Dale's chest tightened. *Gone. She's gone from me. Why did I even talk to Sidney?* A tug on her hand jerked her out of her thoughts.

The music had stopped and everyone else had taken their seats. Dale smoothed the back of her skirt and sat down next to Seth. The ceremony was swift, and Dale missed all of it, her thoughts tangling back on themselves as she scrambled to find the right words to ask Mai to forgive her for believing Sidney's lies.

*

After the wedding, guests helped clear the chairs and Dale's sons pieced together the portable dance floor while the DJ set up his system. As the wedding reception kicked off, the guests helped themselves to various box wines and coolers full of beer and soft drinks.

Mai stood off to the side. The fear and mistrust in Dale's eyes had gutted her. *It's never going to be okay. I was never going to have what I want.* A family. A successful small business. A woman by her side who wanted the same. Nothing radical. And yet it seemed to always be beyond her grasp.

Why? Why is the quintessential house with a white picket fence for everyone but me? She had imagined the scenario with Dale, more times than she cared to think about. And now, because Sidney had fabricated some stupid story, and because Dale was willing to believe her bitter ex-girlfriend rather than trust Mai, she was alone. Again.

Mai tracked Sidney's movements and her stomach roiled as she thought of her game to win Dale back. Disgusted with herself and tired of her pity party, she shoved off from the tree and walked to the closest beer cooler. She lifted the lid and poked among the bottles, looking for a dark brew to match her mood. She found a bottle of stout and dug in her pocket for her multitool and used it to pry off the lid.

The sounds of Tim McGraw's *Set This Circus Down* blasted from the DJ's speakers and Mai turned toward the dance floor. Ida and Jeff slow-danced around the floor. Dale stood off to the side taking video with her phone.

A flurry of movement and the sharp sound of a grunt made her search for the source. Behind her, Noah was locked in a scuffle with Ethan. He sagged in Ethan's arms, his head lolling on his shoulders. Taller and heavier, Ethan forced Noah up against the large oak in the front yard and punched him in the stomach.

Mai dropped her beer and ran toward them. "Hey, asshole! Leave him alone!"

Ethan threw a look over his shoulder as he cocked his fist.

Noah took advantage of the distraction and kneed him in the groin. Ethan grunted and bent at the waist. "Fucking cock-sucker. I'll kill you. Both of you."

Mai shoved him out of the way to check on Noah. His face was wet with blood. Ethan caught her in the jaw with a sucker punch and she stumbled back. She touched trembling fingers to her split lip. They came away wet with blood. She spit to clear her mouth and shook her head to fight the pain.

Noah had wrapped his arms around Ethan and taken the fight to the ground. Mai fought waves of nausea and staggered to where they were fighting. Ethan was on top of Noah, using his thighs to pin Noah's arms to his side. A steady stream of vile hate-filled threats poured from Ethan's mouth as he pummeled Noah's face.

Rage, white-hot and searing, filled Mai. She kicked Ethan in the face. The blow dislodged him. He screamed, fell to his side, and covered his face with his hands. Blood flowed between his fingers. Mai followed him, stepping over Noah, and kicked him in the stomach. He screamed again and curled into a tight ball, his hands clutching his belly. Seeing her opening, Mai raised her foot to stomp his head. A strong arm banded around her waist and hauled her back. She struggled against the iron grip around her waist. "Let me go. Get off me."

"No, Mai. No. It's enough. It's over." Dale's voice broke through her anger.

"Noah. He was hurting Noah," Mai panted. Seth and Thomas picked Noah up off the ground and held him up between them. Chip stood next to them, his face pale. The sounds of a siren in the distance grew closer.

Ethan rolled around on the ground moaning and clutching his stomach. Ida and Jeff and other guests had gathered. "Fucking queers. All of you."

Eli stepped through the crowd. "That's enough." His normally gentle voice was steel. "One more word out of you, Ethan, and there won't be enough for the cops to arrest." He hefted a wooden axe handle across his chest and tapped his palm with it. "Be glad Mai got to you first, instead of me."

With a gentle touch, Dale turned Mai's face to hers. She peered into her eyes. "I'm taking you both to the hospital."

Ethan rose to his knees, swayed once, and then collapsed to his side again. Flashing red lights lit the yard and the siren cut off. The crowd parted as the county sheriff walked up to them.

Sidney pushed through the crowd. "I saw it all, Ben." Her face was flushed and her eyes gleamed and she pointed at Mai and Noah. "Those two jumped Ethan."

"You're a liar." Seth's voice boomed out.

"He's a fag. Everyone knows." Ethan perked up, seizing on Sidney's words. "They did. Fucking queer tried to grab my junk and when I hit him"—he gestured to Mai—"she hit me from behind."

"Liar. You punched me from behind." Noah spoke between cut and bleeding lips. The skin around his right eye was dark-red and swollen.

Chip moved and stood between Noah and Ethan. "He wouldn't touch you if you were the last man on earth, *pinche pendejo*." He clenched both fists. Thomas rested his hand on Chip's shoulder and drew him back.

The sheriff looked between Ethan and Noah, and then cast his gaze to Mai. "How do you figure in all this? I know these two." He pointed at Ethan. "That one especially."

Dale walked forward and took Mai's arm. "She's my partner, and she was saving Noah from Ethan's beating." She held up her phone and clicked the play button. A wobbly video of the bride and groom's first dance began.

Dale zoomed in on the area past the dance floor. Mai's stomach lurched as she watched the part of the fight she had missed. Ethan had stepped out of the shadows and rabbit punched Noah in the back of his head as he had watched Ida and Bill's first dance. Mai shivered and her gut churned, bile rising in her throat. A fraction of an inch lower and Noah could have been killed.

She fought her nausea and continued to watch as Noah feebly lifted his hands to block Ethan's next punch. Staggered by Ethan's surprise attack, Noah never even had chance to throw a punch as Ethan used his face as a punching bag.

Noah's head lolled in the video and his hands hung at his side as Ethan forced him against the tree. The video cut off at the point of Mai's intervention. "I'll swear a statement. And you can have this video." Dale cut her eyes at Sidney. "And unlike some people, I haven't been drinking."

The sheriff scratched his chin and stared at Sidney. "Ain't you the one they fired for sleeping on the job?"

Sidney flushed and took a step back.

The sheriff gestured to Ethan. "I'll take him in my car. He's been in the back before. Y'all meet me at the ER and I'll get your statements." He lifted his chin at Noah. "You're gonna need some stitches."

Noah grimaced. "Yeah." He turned to Ida. "Sorry your wedding got ruined."

Ida hugged him gently. "You have nothing to apologize for." She glared at Ethan. "If I ever see you again, you better hope you see me first." She spit on the ground next to him.

The sheriff hauled Ethan up off the ground, spun him around, and locked handcuffs over his wrists. He loaded him into the back of the squad car and drove away.

Bile rose in Mai's throat and she swayed. "I need some water."

Dale looped her arm around her waist. "Lean on me. Seth, bring Noah. Thomas, pick up a couple of water bottles and some ice packs for the ride."

Seth picked Noah up and carried him. Noah protested feebly for a moment before he relaxed and let his brother carry him to the truck.

"Thank you." Dale hugged Mai to her and pressed a gentle kiss to her temple. "Thank you." The hitch in her voice was the only indicator of how close she was to breaking down.

"I did what anyone would do." Mai touched her swollen lips and the lump on her jaw. "That asshole really hit me."

Dale opened the passenger door for Mai. "No. You did what most people are afraid to do. You put yourself at risk to stop Ethan." Dale's eyes glittered in the pale glow of the truck overhead light. "I owe you an apology."

Mai gazed into Dale's eyes. "It's fine."

"No. It's not. I let Sidney manipulate me. I don't care about your past."

"It's not true by the way. I've never even had a speeding ticket. It was an outright lie."

Dale snorted. "I figured that out the moment I saw her gleeful look when you didn't save me a seat."

Mai shrugged. "I didn't think you wanted to sit with me anyway."

Thomas arrived with the water bottles and two bags of ice. He passed the water to Dale and handed Mai a plastic bag filled with ice. Seth and Thomas settled Noah into the back seat and handed him the other bag of ice. "Grandpa's gonna bring us in his car." They shut the door, and Dale started the engine.

Mai settled into the seat and placed the ice pack against her jaw. "Noah, don't go to sleep. He hit you pretty hard. You keep talking to us."

"So I don't wake up dead?" Noah reached his hand forward. "Can I have some water?"

Mai opened the water bottle and passed it back to Noah. "Yes. You could have a head injury so keep talking."

"You know it's true, Mom, right?" Noah's voice cracked. "I'm queer. Sorry you found out like this."

Dale peered into the rearview mirror to see Noah's face. "You didn't do anything wrong, Noah. I figured you'd tell me when you were ready."

"Ethan's a fucking asshole."

"Language. And you're right."

Noah lay back on the seat. "Mom, I might be sick."

"Under your seat, Mai, is a bag. Pass it to Noah."

Mai handed Noah the bag. His hand trembled when he took it. She shifted her gaze to Dale's profile. "Why was Ethan there anyway?"

Dale blew out a breath. "He was part of the catering crew. I didn't even know he was there, until I saw you all fighting."

"He threatened to kill Noah." Mai blew out a breath. "To kill both of us."

Dale glanced at her. "I heard. So did Ida, and the others."

"Would they swear to it?"

"Like in court?" Noah shifted on the seat and pulled the blanket up higher. "I hope the fucker goes to jail for good this time."

"Yeah. Like in court. This was an assault. And in some places, it would be pursued as a hate crime."

"Language. And I hope the little fucker can't weasel out of it this time. We're in Knox County. That should help." Dale sped up as they made the turn on to the two-lane blacktop road leading to town. "My sister would swear a statement. I think Jeff would. My dad for sure. I'll check with everyone else to see if anyone has more video."

Adrenaline drained from Mai, replaced by fear. Fear for Noah. Fear for herself, and fear Dale would change her mind about them.

"You okay?" Dale's palm on her knee was warm.

"Yeah. Thinking."

"About?"

Mai rested her hand on top of Dale's. "Us. The future." She picked up Dale's hand and kissed the back of her knuckles.

"All right!" Noah's soft cheer from the back seat made Mai laugh and Dale snort.

Chapter Nineteen

Noah pushed away the blanket Dale tucked around him. "Mom, I'm okay. Really."

"You're not. You have a concussion." Dale raked a hand through her hair. "And stitches. Lay back and let me be mom."

Noah sighed dramatically. "I'm bored. This no screens thing is awful."

"Do you want to try some crackers and ginger ale?"

Noah pushed up to sitting. Dale's heart hurt. Anger at Ethan swelled up inside her as she took in Noah's face. Her beautiful boy. She clenched her fists.

"Just the ginger ale. My stomach is still rocky."

"Ice?"

"A little." Noah lay back on the couch.

Dale left him and went to the kitchen. As she was scooping ice from the freezer a sharp rap sounded at the back door. She left the glass on the counter. The knock sounded again before she could get there.

She snatched the door open, unable to hide her annoyance.

Chip stood on the step, with a bouquet of orange mums clenched in his fist. "Um, hi, Ms. Miller. Could I see Noah?"

Dale stepped back. "Of course. He's in the living room."

Chip toed off his trainers and lined them up by the door. "Thank you." He charged around the corner to the living room. Dale took her time making Noah's drink, giving them time alone. The fear and anger in her heart was replaced by wonder at how her son had managed to find a boy as sweet as Chip. She purposely knocked a book off the kitchen table and took her time picking it up on her way back to the living room to give them warning.

Chip sat on the end of the couch with Noah's feet in his lap. He ducked his head. "Noah said he told you."

Dale placed Noah's glass on the coffee table. "He did."

"And it's okay?" Chip looked out from under his bangs. "Like really okay?"

"Why wouldn't it be?" Dale sat back in her chair. "Are you out to your mom?"

Chip huffed out a breath. "My mom knows things about me I don't even know myself. She knows. But my dad doesn't. He's been rabid anti-queer ever since my mom left him."

Dale pressed her lips together. "It won't be easy. But you already know that." She inclined her head toward Noah. "Ethan is out on bond. He's going to be ten times more aggressive because he's stupid. I don't want you, either of you going anywhere alone."

Chip reached over and took Noah's hand. "I'm not going anywhere without him."

Dale turned away from the scene, her heart too full to say anything.

*

The whisper of Dale's footsteps on the carpet startled Mai. She rolled to her back.

"Sorry. I didn't mean to wake you." Dale sat on the edge of the bed.

"I wasn't asleep. I'm tired but I can't fall asleep."

Dale frowned at her. "You were restless last night."

"My jaw hurt, even with the drugs they gave me." She curled on her side. "I'm glad you're here. How's Noah?"

"Snuggled up with Chip."

Mai grinned. "Then you're off nurse duty?"

"I am."

Mai lifted the covers and Dale placed her phone on the nightstand, kicked off her slippers, and slid under the covers.

Mai scooted down and rested her head on Dale's shoulder.

Dale wrapped both arms around Mai. "Do you want to talk about it?"

"No. I don't want to think about it anymore. I can't get the vision of Ethan hitting Noah out of my thoughts."

"I made an appointment for all of us with our family therapist. She helped us a lot after my mom died."

"I'm family?"

Dale kissed the top of Mai's head. "Yep. If you engage in fisticuffs at a family wedding, you are. It's the rules." She squeezed Mai tightly. "I'm incredibly grateful you stayed after I hurt you. You would have been justified to leave after I doubted you."

"No way was I leaving. That's what Sidney wanted. And I'm not intimidated by her stupid ass. I don't chase off easy."

Dale stroked the fine hairs at the back of Mai's neck. "You stepped in. You saved Noah's life."

"I don't know about that." Mai hugged Dale closer.

"I do. You're one of the bravest people I know."

Mai bit her lip. "Do you believe in second chances? Like the universe gives you opportunities to make things right after you've messed up?"

"I hadn't thought about it, why?"

"Do you remember Karen Fairworth? She was your year."

"I think. Tall girl. Played all the sports. Dropped out?"

"That's her."

"And?"

"I was the equipment manager for the basketball team my eighth-grade year. I was there prepping for the next day's game. She was in the gym and had stayed late to practice her free throws. Some kids jumped her in the locker room. I stood by. I froze, didn't jump in. I ran for help. They beat her so badly she lost vision in one eye." Mai gripped the sheet tightly. "If I had stayed, done something, anything besides run for help, I could have made a difference."

"You can't know that. You did what you thought was right at the time. You were thirteen. You have to let it go. It's a long way from thirteen to forty." Dale rubbed her back in slow circles.

"You keep doing that and I'm going to fall back asleep."

"A nap sounds good right now."

"When do you need to check on Noah again?"

"At two. My phone will beep."

The warmth of Dale's body and her calming touch soothed her, and Mai let her eyes drift closed.

Chapter Twenty

Mai poured the hot water over the grounds in the coffee press. While it steeped, she leaned against the counter and wrote out her grocery list. A key scraped in the back door lock. Thomas opened the door. "It smells good in here." He unlaced his shoes, toed them off, and placed them next to the door.

"Is there enough for me too?" Seth entered the kitchen from the basement. He scratched at the stubble on his chin.

Mai raised her eyebrow. "Why are both of you here early?" The hairs on the back of her neck stood up.

Thomas flushed. "We wanted to talk to you."

Seth drew three cups from the cabinet. "Yeah." He placed the cups next to the press.

Mai pressed the grounds down and poured three cups of coffee. "Is this where you tell me to leave your mom alone? Ask me my intentions?" She leveled her gaze at the two of them. "Because I'm not going anywhere. You can shove off if that's your mission. Your mom is a grown woman who is more than capable of telling me to hit the bricks if she wants me to leave. And I'm an honorable person, no matter what filth Sidney has been spreading." Seth and Thomas's mouths gaped. "And she is the only one who I'm going to listen to, so if that's your agenda, kindly fuck off."

"Woah!" Thomas pushed his glasses up on his nose. "That is so not what we wanted to talk about."

"We wanted to ask if you would help us do something nice for her birthday."

Mai flushed. "Oh damn. I'm sorry." She rubbed the back of her neck. "I'm sorry, guys."

Seth picked up his cup and sipped his coffee. "But since you brought it up. You're not going to break Mom's heart, right? I mean you're in it for real, aren't you?"

"I am. What did you have in mind for her birthday?"

Thomas sat down next to Seth. "You love Mom?"

Mai rolled her eyes. "I haven't said that to her yet, so please let's leave it at I care, okay?"

Thomas pulled his glasses off and pulled a lens cloth from his shirt pocket and cleaned them. "Look, I'm not a warm fuzzy feeling kinda guy, and even I can see it's more than that, but whatever." He sipped his coffee and leaned back in his chair.

"We want you to help to surprise her with a super-special dinner and a cake. She always did great birthday parties for us when we were kids. Even when we were flat broke she made them special." Seth frowned. "Last year Sidney got in the way, insisted she take Mom to a fancy restaurant." His eyes grew dark. "I don't know what happened, but Mom broke up with her that night."

Mai pursued her lips. "Can't say I'm unhappy about that. But I hate your mom had a horrible birthday. I know how that feels." Mai blinked away the memory of her mother forgetting her nineteenth birthday. The last one she ever spent at home. Twenty-one years later and it still stung. She tapped her finger to her lips. "What is her favorite kind of cake?"

"Yellow with chocolate icing." Thomas picked up an apple and bit into it.

"You guys planning Mom's birthday without me?" Noah's indignant whisper startled them.

"No, Tiny Tot, we were just getting started."

The bruises on Noah's cheeks and around his eyes shone yellow-purple against his pale skin under the fluorescent kitchen lights.

"Don't push it, Noah. You're supposed take it easy for another two weeks." Mai poured Noah a glass of apple juice and placed it on the table.

Noah sat down heavily in the kitchen chair and rubbed his fingers over the cartoon figure of SpongeBob decorated on the side of the glass. "Who'd have thought I'd miss school so much?"

Mai held up her notepad. "Okay, so far we have yellow cake with chocolate frosting. What else should we make?"

"Mom used to make us pizza all the time for our birthdays."

"Yeah, but that was for us. What would Mom like?" Thomas sipped his coffee.

"French onion soup to start, with homemade bread. Salad." Seth shifted in his seat. "That's what she orders when we go out for Grandpa's birthday."

"Can we think more fancy?" Noah huffed. "We make that for her all the time."

"What do you think she would like, Mai?" Noah gulped his juice.

Mai tapped the pen against her lip. "She loved the ravioli we made Noah. What if we do three different kinds of ravioli and a salad?"

"Cool." Seth frowned. "I think Thomas and I can make the cake."

Mai grinned. "If you can build a house, Seth, you can bake a cake. I'll leave the cake to you two. Noah and I will make the dinner. How are we going to work the surprise?"

Thomas sat back and crossed his arms. "I'll get Grandpa in on it. He's good at faking Mom out."

Love, bright and warm, washed over Mai. She loved this family. These young men who wanted to do something special for their mother. She leaned back against the counter. The sense of being included in the plans for Dale's surprise birthday warmed her, made her catch her breath. Family.

*

Dale drew her fingers along the valley over Mai's spine, stopping to swirl her fingertip over the dimple above her ass. "I almost fell out of my truck the day I watched you change in your car." She shifted her hips and rolled them against the round muscle of Mai's ass and skated her palms over the broad planes of Mai's back.

Mai reached back and stroked the outside of Dale's calf. "I couldn't believe you were early. I planned on being dressed before you got there."

Dale leaned down and kissed the nape of Mai's neck. "I'm glad I was early for once."

She stretched out over Mai and rubbed her nipples along her back before she lowered herself with a groan. Mai arched her hips under her, and Dale ground her clit against her ass. She nibbled her neck and rolled to the side. Mai turned toward her.

With one leg over Mai's thighs to hold her in place, Dale teased a finger over Mai's stiff clit. She edged her, slicking her fingers over the hard knot of her clit, drawing back each time Mai's breathing shifted, signaling she was close to coming.

She pressed her lips against the shell of Mai's ear. "You're beautiful. Every time I touch you, I can hardly believe you're in my bed."

Mai panted. "I love being in your bed. I love being in your life."

Dale pushed two fingers inside and stroked gently, drawing out Mai's orgasm until she shuddered and shouted into the pillow as she came.

Dale shifted and rolled her over to look into her face.

Mai leaned up and kissed her. She broke their kiss and gazed into Dale's eyes. "I love you."

Dale's breath hitched. She had known this was coming. Had sensed it herself. Had opened her mouth to say something in the weeks since Noah's attack. She cupped Mai's face in both hands. She hesitated a beat too long.

Mai's withdrawal was so sharp it seemed physical and her gaze slid away from Dale's. "It's fine if you don't feel the same. I wanted you to know." She broke free from Dale's grip and rolled away from her. She scooted to the edge of the bed, shoved off, and stalked to the bathroom. The click of the door lock echoed in the room.

Why didn't I say it back? Why can't I say it? Because every time I say I love you in a relationship it goes pear-shaped. And she's never going to be satisfied here. With us. With me. The sound of the shower running made her drag herself from her bed. She grabbed the bathroom doorknob and turned it. Locked. She had locked her out. And who could blame her? Dale must seem like everyone else who wanted Mai for what she was, not who she was.

Dale grabbed her jeans off the floor and pulled her multitool from its pouch. Using the punch, she opened the door.

"I know it's your house, but I locked it for some privacy." Mai's hollow voice called from behind the shower glass.

Dale yanked open the shower door, stepped into the tub, and pulled Mai into her arms.

"Damn it, Mai. Give a woman a chance to respond before you bolt out of her bed. I care about you. I've cared about you since we had our first argument."

Mai kissed her and Dale clung to her as Mai's kisses swept away her fears. She cupped Dale's neck, her eyes dark under her thick brows. "Don't say it if you don't mean it."

"You're the best thing ever walked into my life. I want you to be with you."

The water cooled. Dale shivered and Mai shut off the flow.

Mai stepped out, grabbed a towel, and passed it on to Dale. She dried herself off briskly. "Come on."

Dale followed Mai to the bed. Clasping her shoulders, Mai used her body weight to encourage Dale to lay back. Mai kneeled at the bedside. She kissed the inside of Dale's thigh and Dale let her legs fall open. Her wet tongue slid along and over her skin.

Mai blew her warm breath over Dale's clit before she licked it. Nuzzling the inside of her leg before she kissed the crease of her thigh, she moved back to her center and thrust her tongue deep and then swirled it over her clit again. Dale grabbed the sheets with both hands as Mai took her time and brought her off.

*

"This is amazing." Mai shifted the hard hat back to look up at the ceiling of the restaurant. "You saved the copper ceiling? It looks like it did when I was a kid."

Dale basked in Mai's happiness. "There wasn't as much water damage as we thought down here." She pressed her lips together in a thin line. "Upstairs, we had to gut most of it."

Mai walked over to the frame for the bar and leaned on it. "I know you did what you could."

"Come with me." Dale's gut tightened as she hoped Mai would approve of the changes she had made to the upstairs apartment. They took the elevator up. "It will hold up to eight hundred pounds. I checked the recommended specs for potential electric wheelchair use." Dale pressed the button to open the door. "This keypad can be programed to operate the elevator remotely."

Mai stepped out into the open floor plan. The wall dividing the apartments was gone. A long kitchen bar separated the living room and kitchen.

She ran her hand along the reclaimed barn wood countertop and whistled. "This is much more than I imagined."

"The countertop and everything are ADA compliant. I asked a few friends with mobility issues what they would want and incorporated their suggestions."

Mai turned to her. "Thank you. So much. This fantastic."

Dale took her hand. "Come see the bedrooms."

Mai followed Dale down the short hall to the bedrooms.

"There will be two bedrooms with full bathrooms. Both will have in roll-in showers, with benches and grab bars. I know it doesn't look like much now but as soon as the wiring and the plumbing rough-in is complete we can get started on the rest of it."

Dale opened the door and Mai stepped in.

Mai turned in a slow circle. "This will be perfect for Yvonne and me."

Dale looked away briefly to smooth her grimace at the reminder Mai would leave her home as soon as the renovation was complete. "I'm sure."

"You made a skylight? Wow. It's wonderful. It was always dark in here growing up."

"Since the roof needed to be rebuilt anyway it was easy." Dale flushed with Mai's delight.

"I can't wait to lie in bed and look at the sky change." Mai swept her hard hat off and cupped Dale's chin. "With you." She kissed her and Dale rested her hands on her hips and tugged her closer, making full contact with Mai's firm body.

"You're violating safety rules." She smiled against Mai's mouth. "Pretty stiff penalty for that."

Mai rocked into Dale's body. "I'm sure we can work something out."

"Maybe we can." Dale nipped her lip and stepped back.

Mai put her hard hat back on. "Is Yvonne's room the same?"

"Exactly. No sister fights over who gets the skylight."

Mai clasped both of Dale's hands in hers. "Thank you, for all of this. I'm impressed. It's more than I ever dreamed of."

Dale nodded, not trusting herself to speak. She'd made Mai happy, ecstatic even. But the reality of Mai moving out of her home, and potentially out of her life, twisted a knife in her gut and squeezed her heart.

She dropped Mai's hands and stepped back and glanced away from her sparkling eyes. "Let me show you the rest of it. I need you to make some decisions."

Dale turned and walked away from Mai, wondering when it would be the last time. Of course, she would leave. It had only been a temporary arrangement to save Mai money, and to help Dale. And now? Now Dale didn't know what they were. Family? Friends? Friends with hella benefits? She finished the tour and made notes of Mai's choices for paint colors and tile for the kitchen and bathroom.

Mai bubbled with excitement as they walked down the stairs. "I can't wait to be here. I've been working on the menus with Sally and the folks at the co-op. Do you have an estimate when it will be complete?"

Dale clutched her clipboard to her chest. "Some of it will depend on the city inspector's schedule. And then once the building is cleared, you'll need to check with the health department about their inspections."

Mai sighed. "Hurry up and wait, as my mom used to say."

Dale gestured to the outlines of the equipment painted on the floor with fluorescent paint. "This is according to the layout you approved. Would you walk it and let me know if you still want it this way? Once we plumb it and put the wiring in it will get expensive to change anything."

Mai moved around the kitchen space and Dale stood off to the side and imagined her in chef's whites working the open kitchen. She found the concentration on her face as she prepared an imaginary meal fascinating. She moved across the kitchen like a dancer. Mai stopped mid-stride and a frown crossed her face.

"Something wrong?"

Mai raised her gaze to Dale's face. "A memory. My mom. She used to run the meals. We never had waitresses. Yvonne wasn't steady enough to carry a tray." Mai pointed to the bright-orange line on the floor that indicated where the pass-through would be built. "Yvonne sat there, she answered the phone, took the orders, and ran the cash register." Mai glanced up, her eyes bright. "It was hell on Friday and Saturday nights, but I'd give everything I have to have my mom yelling at me to hurry up with the dish I was taking too much time to plate."

Dale walked to Mai and gathered her in her arms. "I get that. Even the hard times are precious once someone's gone."

Chapter Twenty-One

Mai scrolled through her email box. A starred email from her agent popped to the top of the list. Her chest tightened as she read the offer. She sent back her reply and lay back on the couch.

Money. A cushion for the first year they would be open. And maybe enough to take Dale on a real vacation. If she could convince her. She grimaced. Three months away. And Charlene.

Her gut churned as she thought of Charlene's last attempt to seduce her after they had split. Mai swiped at the beads of sweat popping out on her brow. *I can do this. I'm professional. And the money. The money would be sweet. Three months away from Dale. Does she love me? She cares. What does that mean? Maybe she'll jump right back into Hit Me Up the second I'm gone?*

Mai covered her face with both hands. *Noah. I'm going to have to tell him. It will be worse than telling Dale. If I say yes to the special will there be anything to come back to if I do? Will it be worth it? Will I lose everything chasing after money?*

The crash and bang of the back door startled her.

"Hey, Mai? You home?" Noah called from the kitchen.

"In here." Mai sat up on the couch and rested her elbows on her knees and her chin in her hands.

Noah sat next to her and peeled a banana. "You okay?"

"Yeah. No. I got an offer. To go back and do a special. It's only eight shows."

Noah chewed and swallowed his bite of banana before he spoke. "What about Mom?"

Mai fidgeted with her shirt buttons. "You have to stop shipping your mom and me. Your mom's not in the same place I am." Mai's chest squeezed as she thought about her confession to Dale, her "I love you" unreturned and Dale's nebulous "I care about you."

Thomas finished his banana before he spoke. His eyes were hooded and his expression flat. "You gonna do it?"

"I haven't given them an answer yet."

"It'd be a lot of money, wouldn't it?" He looked away from Mai.

"Yeah. But money isn't everything."

Noah snorted. "Only people who have it ever say that." He stood up and walked back toward the kitchen.

Mai watched him walk away and the hunched set of his shoulders and cursed herself for ever agreeing to the arrangement with Dale. Noah was right. She could no more walk away from earning money than fly. Too many nights of sleeping in her car, and making the choice between paying bills and eating, for her to ever walk away from a paycheck. Even with more money in the bank than she could spend in her life, she still worried about every dime. She rubbed at her chest as an ache had settled there.

She lay back on the couch and clasped her hands over her stomach. Clouds scuttled across the sky, plunging the room into gray shadows. Mai stared unseeing at the ceiling as she turned the last six months over in her thoughts. How could she walk away from a large paycheck and the possibility of more?

Money in the bank was the only sure thing, the only security Mai had ever known. The slam of a cabinet door followed by the crash of metal pans brought her to her feet. "Noah?"

Mai rounded the corner and came to a full stop. Noah stood in the middle of the floor. An assortment of pans and pots spilled across the floor. The cabinet door stood ajar, half off its hinges.

"Sorry," he mumbled.

"You okay?" Mai kneeled next to him to pick up the cookware.

"Just peachy." Noah turned away from her. He placed the stack of pans he was holding on the counter.

Mai gathered the few remaining pots and placed them next to the pans. Noah moved away and grabbed his jacket off the hook. Wordlessly he turned to the door.

"You have practice?" Mai glanced at the calendar next to the door.

"No." Noah walked out and closed the door gently behind him.

Mai turned back to the jumble of pots and pans. A too perfect reminder of the chaos her leaving would create.

Chapter Twenty-Two

The motor on the dust collector hummed in the background, muffled by Dale's hearing protectors. She turned the heart-shaped box in her hands and smoothed the edges until she was satisfied with the shape. The lines of the lacewood made a delicate pattern over the top and sides of the box. Dale pressed the floor switch to turn the sander and the dust collector off. She placed the box on the workbench.

The fading sunlight filtering through the trees drew deep shadows over the drive. The last few oak leaves sounded their death rattle before they let go of the tree's branches as a blustery wind sent them scattering over the lawn. Dale sat down and contemplated her work. The sweeping curves she had shaped with the sander gave depth to the box. *Will she like it? Is it too much? It's too much. Too early. She'll go to New York. Who wants an insta-family?*

Dale turned her back on her project and set about tidying her work space. She swept up stray wood chips from the floor and deposited them into the bin. The only thing left to do was to saw the box open. A critical step. A sloppy cut would ruin all the other work that had gone into building the box. Once the two halves were separated it was only a matter of a bit more sanding, finishing, and then adding the hinges and the latch.

She'd cut open hundreds of boxes in her time in the workshop but this time it wasn't merely a wood and glue creation. Her gift to Mai was all the things she struggled to say. It was as if her own heart lay on the bench instead of the clever box she had created.

What if she takes the job? What if she doesn't come back? At least we had what we had. Dale picked up the box and carried it to the bandsaw. After adjusting it for the cut she wanted, she replaced her hearing protectors and flipped the switch. The subtle vibration of the saw transferred through the wood. Dale focused on the line of her cut and let out the breath she had been holding when the heart split into two.

She turned off the saw. The two halves cleaved perfectly in her hands. The inside of the box was as she had envisioned it with the lacewood grain pattern highlighting the unique shape of the box. Dale lined up the two halves and inspected the edge. A straight and solid match. A touch of sanding with ultrafine sandpaper and it would be ready for the oil finish she had planned. She ran her thumb over the curve of the box.

"Came out better than I thought it would," Eli called from the door.

"Thanks, Dad." Dale placed the two halves on the workbench.

Eli scratched his beard. "You in love with her?"

Dale sat down on the tall stool next to the workbench. "Does it show?"

"Only if you've got eyes." Eli walked over to Dale. "You look awful blue for someone in love."

"Noah told me she's had an offer to do an eight-week special. She'd be gone for three months."

"And? It'll take that long for you to finish the renovation."

"She'll be working with her ex." Dale drummed her fingers on the workbench. "Her much younger and very sexy beautiful ex."

"You're missing the key word in that sentence." Eli leaned on his elbows on the workbench. "Her 'ex.'"

Dale barked out a laugh. "You and I both know that is no guarantee nothing will happen. What if she wants Mai back?"

Eli stacked the two halves of the heart together. "So what if she does? Mai seems solid. Does she know how you feel about her?"

Dale pursed her lips. "No. Yes. She told me she loved me, and I freaked and didn't say it back. Just said I cared for her." She flushed as she remembered the aftermath of her apology.

Eli tapped the top of the box. "This is your way of doing it? Giving her your heart?"

"It's silly, isn't it?" She snatched the box up. "It's childish. I should be able to say it."

Eli reached out and touched the back of her hand. "Not silly, daughter, scary as fuck, but not silly to be afraid to say it. But, box or no, you need to tell her how you feel."

Dale lifted her gaze to his. "I know." She placed the box gently on the workbench.

*

The grocery store was sparsely populated on Thursday afternoon. Noah pushed a grocery cart ahead of Mai. Thomas and Seth trailed behind her with another cart.

Mai tore the grocery list in half. "This will go much faster if we split up. Call me if you have questions about the list. Meet you by the registers when we're done." She handed half the list to Thomas and Seth.

"Thanks for doing this. Mom always made our birthdays special. Even when we were broke as hell."

Mai patted Seth's shoulder. "I'm happy to do it." Thomas pushed the cart ahead and Seth jogged after him.

Noah popped a wheelie with their cart. "I bet we can beat them to the front."

"Easy, tiger, we need to take our time, so we don't forget anything. And we have more items to procure." She waved the list in the air and led the way to the first aisle.

Noah chewed his lip, a pensive expression on his face.

"What?" Mai placed two dozen eggs in the front of the cart.

"What if Mom's mad we spent the grocery money on her birthday? This going to put us way over budget for the month."

Mai rested her palm on his shoulder. "This is my treat. You all have been more than gracious housing me. I would have been in some crappy hotel or short-term rental. This is on me."

"Mom sure liked it when you bought the flowers." He looked at her from under his shaggy fringe of hair. "She likes you. Like a lot, I think."

Mai tilted her head at Noah. "I know. I like your mom too."

Noah straightened. "Are you going to tell her?"

"Tell her what?"

"How you feel." Noah placed a container of sweet cream into the cart.

Mai settled a block of cheese next to the eggs and studied the list and avoided Noah's eyes.

"Not yet," she lied.

"You should tell her. Soon."

"Noah, what are you not saying?"

"Mom has a date. On Saturday. She wants me to spend the night at Chip's. And she asked Seth to sleep somewhere else that night." He smirked. "That's code for her not wanting to worry about us when she gets home."

Mai stomach clenched hard. She hadn't asked for exclusivity. She'd assumed. And now she had to deal with it. *What the hell? You would think telling someone you loved them might make them at least not date anyone for a while. Fuck her.* Her decision to expose her feelings to Dale settled firmly in her gut. *She doesn't love me. She cares. But not enough to wait until I leave. Ugh. Charlene all over again.*

"Did you get the nutmeg? Your jar is older than you are." Mai inclined her head toward the spice aisle.

Noah frowned. "I guess you don't want to talk about it."

"You guessed right." Mai rolled the edge of the shopping list. "Your mom's free to do whatever she wants." *Damn it.*

*

"Come on, Dad. We're going to be late." Dale rattled her car keys.

"Hold on a minute. I'm in the middle of texting with Ms. Zettler."

"Do it in the truck!"

"Reception's terrible. And you can wait for me."

"I'll be in the truck." She strode out of the back door and across the yard.

After entering the truck, Dale pulled out her phone. A text from Noah. She opened it.

Mom. You need to come home. Right now. Bring Granddad.

Dale leaned on the horn, not letting up until her father appeared.

"What in hell is wrong with you? I said I would be a minute."

"Get in Dad. Noah needs me, us."

Eli clambered into car, barely getting his seatbelt clipped before Dale peeled out of the drive, throwing gravel.

"Did he say why?"

Dale tossed her phone in his direction. "No. Text him back and tell him we're coming." Her hands ached where she gripped the wheel.

The normally twenty-minute drive to her home only took ten. The house was dark, and Dale struggled to breathe as rising panic swamped her.

She pulled in the drive, shut the truck down, and yanked the keys from the ignition. Eli scrambled to keep up with her.

The door hung open and Dale shoved through it, sending it crashing against the frame, and stormed into the dark kitchen.

"Surprise!" Noah, Seth, Thomas, and Mai shouted.

Dale clutched her chest. "You assholes. You scared me to death."

The boys and Mai broke out into laugher and Eli leaned against the counter. "We got her, boys."

Dale eyed the "happy birthday" streamers and balloons hanging about the dining room. She rolled her eyes, and then laughed with them. "I almost peed my pants."

Noah stepped forward and gave her hug. "Sorry we scared you."

Dale ruffled his hair. The wonderful smell of homemade ravioli filled the kitchen.

Seth waved a bottle of sparkling non-alcoholic cider in one hand and a growler of beer in the other. "What do you want to drink, Mom?"

"After that I'm ready for a tall glass of beer." She hung her purse by the door.

"I'll take a beer too." Eli walked over to the stove and lifted the lid on the pan of sauce. "Smells divine." A knock at the door made him turn.

Thomas opened the door.

Ms. Zettler stood on the porch with a bouquet of roses and baby's breath. "Am I late?"

Eli stepped forward. "No. Right on time. We wanted you to miss the swearing." He kissed her cheek. "Let me get your coat."

Ms. Zettler shrugged out of her coat and he hung it up.

Dale eyed the couple, her heart envious of the obvious affection between them. She sensed Mai's eyes on her and turned in her direction. Mai held out a glass of beer. "Your beer." Her gaze settled on Dale. "I got the coffee stout." Their fingers grazed each other's as she took the glass from Mai.

A liquid heat flowed from her touch and directly to her belly. Later. After the family left, Dale decided, she was going to punish Mai in the most delicious way she could think of for helping the boys pull off the surprise party. Mai raised an eyebrow as if she could read Dale's naughty inner thoughts and, in that moment, there was no one else in the room.

"Um, Mom, do you want to open your present?"

Dale frowned at Thomas. "You didn't have to get me anything. This party is plenty."

Thomas guided her to a dining room chair. "Wait here."

Seth and Thomas scurried from the room. Noah and Mai huddled in the corner, their voices pitched too low for Dale to hear what they were saying.

The back door swung wide and the boys carried a Maloof style rocking chair with a yellow bow tied around it and deposited it in front of Dale.

She ran her fingers over the polished wood. "You made this?"

"Granddad helped. But we all worked on it." They turned the chair so that the bottom of the seat was up. Burned into the wood was the inscription: *To Mom, with love, Seth, Thomas, and Noah.*

Dale blinked back tears as her sons placed the chair to rights. "Come here." They crowed around her chair and hugged her. "Thank you. It's precious."

She caught Mai's gaze and held it. Mai's half smile made her heart squeeze tight. This. A family. And a partner who understood, who helped her kids, instead of trying to always get rid of them. Someone like Mai.

"All right, break it up, this old man is hungry." Eli winked at Dale and she let go of her sons.

"Noah, come help me. Guys, set the table and someone get Ms. Zettler a drink." Mai pulled the plates from the oven where they had been warming.

Thomas and Seth moved the rocking chair to the living room and then moved the table back in place. Noah set the table with napkins folded like swans and silverware.

"Anything I can do to help?" Ms. Zettler set her glass of cider down on the counter.

Mai handed her a basket with crusty slices of bread. "If you could put this on the table would be great."

Dale sipped her beer and Eli sat next to her. "You okay?"

She patted his arm. "Yeah. Got a bit weepy with the gift. It's amazing."

"Thomas and Seth built it and Noah did the finishing. They worked on it for months. Mai helped them with the food, but they made most of it. Seth made the cake." Eli sat back in his chair and took a sip of his beer. "You gonna give her the box?"

Dale's gaze settled on Mai. "Yes."

"When? Should I take the boys back to my house?" His gaze rested on Ms. Zettler.

"Not if you had plans. I've got something planned for next weekend."

Eli leaned forward and clasped her arm. "Don't chicken out."

Dale lifted her shoulders and let them fall, straightening her posture. "I won't."

Eli raised his eyebrow.

"Promise, I won't chicken out."

Mai settled two steaming platters of ravioli in the center of the table. Noah brought another platter of ravioli and a bowl of tomato sauce alongside the other platters. Seth and Thomas filled everyone's glasses.

Mai stepped back and raised her glass. "To Dale, happy birthday, from your assholes."

"Language," the entire crew yelled before they all took a sip of their beverages.

Chapter Twenty-Three

Mai scrubbed at the stubborn dough plastered to the side of the bowl. Dirty dishwater splashed over the side of the sink and wet the front of her pants. She scowled as the soapy water soaked through the fabric of her jeans. Mai focused on her task as thorny vines of jealousy twisted and grew low in her belly and wrapped around her heart. *No. I've no right to feel or expect anything. She "cares." So what. Doesn't mean she has to be exclusive.*

Dale had disappeared into her room as soon as Noah left with Chip. At loose ends, Mai had tried to distract herself by reading a new mystery she had borrowed from the library. After reading the same page four times she had given up and did what she always did when her heart was aching: she baked. A sour cherry pie cooled on the rack. She washed the last of her baking tools and placed them in the dish drainer.

The tip-tap of Dale's pumps on the linoleum along with the faint scent of Dale's signature lemon verbena perfume announced her arrival in the kitchen. Mai rested her chin on her chest and closed her eyes, not wanting to see what fabulous and sexy outfit Dale had on. *Not the red dress. Please let it not be the red dress.*

Dale wrapped her arms around her waist and Mai started. Dale pressed a kiss to the back of her neck. Mai trembled in her embrace.

"Don't." Mai's voice wobbled. "I'm not okay with an open relationship. If that's what you want. I can't. I'm sorry. I'm not wired that way."

Dale hugged her and rested her chin on her shoulder. "Neither am I."

Mai wriggled free of her arms and turned to her. "So, what is this?" She waved her hand over Dale's outfit, only to realize she was wearing a robe and stockings and heels. "Oh."

Dale smirked. "Oh. What were you thinking?"

Mai flushed. "Noah said you had a date."

"I do." Dale stepped closer and looped her arms around Mai's neck. "With you." She played with the hair at the back of Mai's neck. "Unless you're busy?"

Mai rested her hands on Dale's waist. "Why didn't you tell me?"

Dale mouth lifted in a sly smile. "And spoil the surprise?" She kissed Mai, her mouth like honeyed wine. "Come to bed." She took Mai's hand and led her to the bedroom.

"Sit." She pointed to the mattress.

Mai toed off her shoes and left them by the door. She sauntered to the bed, sat, and leaned back on her elbows. Her gaze traveled over Dale's satin-wrapped frame. Her broad shoulders and mouth-watering curvy hips above her long legs set off by her elegant pumps had Mai wanting to kneel at her feet and worship every inch of her. Dale shook out her hair. The golden-brown strands shone in the afternoon sunlight.

"I have something for you." She pinned Mai in place with her gaze as she untied the belt to her robe.

The dark-blue satin drifted open. Dale shrugged out of it and tossed it aside. The bright-green lace Merry

Widow corset framed and lifted her breasts. Matching lace-up panties and wide straps held silk stockings in place and completed the outfit. Pinup model perfection, all for Mai.

Dale placed her hands on her hips and her predatory gaze landed on Mai. "Like what you see?

"Oh yeah." Mai's hands opened and closed as she reached for Dale.

Dale lifted her index finger and waved it back and forth. "No. You are way overdressed for this. Clothes off. Now."

Mai yanked at her shirt, undid three buttons, and pulled it over her head along with her undershirt. She stood up and popped the buttons on her jeans before she snatched them off along with her briefs and socks. Naked, she sat back down on the mattress.

Mesmerized, she devoured the sight of Dale's ass covered by the lace-up panties as she walked to the dresser. After a saucy glance over her shoulder, Dale lifted a pair of black metal handcuffs from the top of the dresser. She let them dangle from her fingers as she walked back to the bed. With one hand in the middle of Mai's chest she pushed her back on to the mattress.

Mai scooted across the bed until her feet were off the floor. Dale drew the handcuffs over her chest, the metal cold against her skin. Her nipples hardened to tight points. Dale sucked one into her mouth and swirled her tongue over the stiff tip as she placed the handcuffs to the side.

"Close your eyes." She kissed Mai's eyes closed.

Mai's breath ratcheted up as the mattress shifted as Dale left the bed. The brush of her pumps on the carpet and the sound of the closet door opening and closing had

Mai's mind racing. The bed moved under her again. Dale's stocking-clad thighs touched her bare skin. A weight landed on her stomach.

"Open your eyes."

Mai opened her eyes to a box wrapped in plain brown paper. "For me?"

"For us." Dale's gaze burned. "Open it."

Mai ripped the paper open and pushed it aside. The outside of the box held no clues to the contents. She tore the lid off. Nestled in the box was a thick dual-headed dildo and bottle of lube. Mai traced her fingers over the toy. "I've seen these. I've never played with one."

Dale lifted the toy clear of the box and placed it on Mai's belly. "Me either." She placed the bottle of lube on the nightstand and lifted the box away.

When she leaned down to place the box on the floor next to the bed, Mai slid a finger under the edge of her lace panties. Dale gasped and Mai continued tickling the edge of her labia. After gathering the wet heat on the tip of her finger she swept it over Dale's fat clit.

Dale gasped. "Oh. You. Stop. Not yet." She moved away from Mai's touch and pushed her hair back from her face.

Mai drew her hand away and licked her sweetness-slicked fingers. "Why?" She smoothed her hand over the panties and silk stockings.

"Because I have a plan." Dale kissed her and laced their fingers together. She tugged Mai's lip between her teeth and then soothed the nip with her tongue. With quick movements she cuffed Mai to the lower rail of the headboard. Mai wiggled and settled her hips on the bed. A trickle of wet heat flowed from her and she pressed her thighs together.

"No gag?" Mai shifted her gaze to Dale's panties.

"We have the house to ourselves. And I want your mouth available." Dale moved off the bed, untied the lace underwear, and let it fall away. She was shaved bare. With a languid sweep of her fingers she touched her clit. She drew her glistening fingertips over Mai's lips. Mai opened her mouth to suck her fingers. Dale teased them in and out of her mouth.

Mai moaned and rattled the handcuffs against the bed rail. "Please. Let me taste you. Please."

"Later." Dale mounted the bed and shoved a pillow under Mai's head. "Comfortable?"

"Yes." Mai strained against the cuffs, her hands opening and closing. "Please. Sit on my face. Please. Let me make you come."

Dale tossed her hair back and leaned down. "Patience." Her hair hid her face as she moved lower to lick and suck Mai's breasts.

Electric arcs of pleasure lit Mai up. Her clit ached and she squirmed under Dale's attentions. "Touch me. Please. Please."

Dale flattened her palm and cupped Mai. She pushed two fingers inside. "So wet. But let's make sure."

She sat up and poured lube into her palm; held it a moment to warm it. She pursed her lips and sucked Mai's clit as she pumped her fingers in and out to spread the lube. Mai arched and trembled beneath her.

Dale sucked her clit relentlessly. Given the freedom to make noise, Mai shouted as she came hard. The metal of the cuffs bit into her skin as she curled her hips into Dale's mouth seeking more.

"Hmmm. Gorgeous." Dale swirled her fingers inside Mai, setting off a series of aftershocks. "Now you're wet enough." She sat up and picked up the toy from beside Mai and held it up. "Don't know if I want to fuck you first or go for a ride."

Mai panted. "Ride me. Please." She spread her legs wide. "Put it in me. Please."

Dale leaned over her, her hair curtaining them. She traced a finger over Mai's cheek. "Since you asked nicely." She pushed the tip of the short side of the toy against Mai's slick folds.

The pressure increased to the edge of pain even as Mai craved more. "Oh, wait. Give me a moment." Mai slowed her breathing and closed her eyes.

Dale sat up and rubbed slow circles over Mai's clit. "This should help."

Mai focused on her touch, willing her body to relax. "Okay. I'm okay. More."

Dale jacked her clit between her finger and thumb slowly as she pushed the dildo forward until it was seated. Mai's body clenched around the shaft as it settled against her g-spot. Dale slid her hand over the shaft, smearing lube along its length. The vibrations along the shaft and the ridges of the toy brushed against Mai's clit and she shuddered through another orgasm. "This is crazy good."

Dale's eyes gleamed. "It's about to be better." She straddled Mai, held herself open, and sank on to the lubed shaft. Her eyes closed as she seated the toy deep inside. Mai panted, planted her feet on the bed, and arched her hips, thrusting into Dale, the movement sending a strong wave of pleasure through her as the toy pressed against her g-spot.

Dale cupped Mai's breasts and thumbed her nipples. She rocked her hips and rose up on her knees enough for Mai to watch the toy disappear again as she lowered herself. The twin sensations of fucking Dale as she was being fucked herself made her thrash her hips. "Oh, faster. Go faster. I need..." Mai licked her lips. "Please. I need more."

Dale leaned down, pressing her full length against Mai, her weight comforting, and Mai lost herself in the feeling of being taken, owned, possessed by Dale.

Dale kissed her, thrusting her tongue into Mai's mouth in time with each roll of her hips. The angle of the toy brushed against her clit with Dale's rhythmic movements. Mai closed her eyes as pleasure blossomed outward from her center. Dale was her world. Time ceased as they rode the waves of pleasure, each thrust and roll bringing them closer to their ultimate destination. Dale's deep groans and sharp cries of ecstasy filled Mai's ears.

"I'm close. Open your eyes. I want to see you when you come." Dale's voice was rough and her warm breath tickled Mai's ear.

Mai opened her eyes. Dale clasped her face and leaned her brow against her forehead. Their gazes locked and Mai crested with a shout, followed by Dale, her hips gyrating wildly as she rode out her pleasure. Mai's shoulders ached as she pulled hard against the headboard, the chain of the cuffs rattling as they plunged headlong into the abyss of pleasure together.

*

Dale held Mai's gaze as she came, her body clenching around the toy. Entranced by the dark depths of Mai's eyes she held tight to what she saw there. Desire. Satisfaction. Love. Mai had said she loved Dale and, in that moment, as she opened her body to Dale, it was there in her eyes. Dale picked up the key from the side table and unlocked the handcuffs. Mai mouthed her nipples through the stiff fabric of the corset as she leaned over her. The instant her hands were free she clutched Dale's shoulders and rolled them so that she was on top. Dale whimpered as the toy slid free.

"Easy baby. I got you." Mai braced herself on her arms and lowered her hips. "Help me?"

Dale reached between them, spread her legs wide, and guided the tip to her entrance. Mai shifted her hips and filled her in one long slow stroke. Dale inhaled sharply, lifted her legs, and wrapped them around Mai's thin hips. She reached and looped her arms around her neck. "Give it to me. All of it."

Mai bared her teeth and pulled back until the toy was almost clear of Dale's body before she thrust forward. Dale hummed. "Like that. Oh yes." She smoothed her hands over the muscles of Mai's strong back.

"Going to take my time."

Dale mock pouted. "Oh no. Anything but that." She rocked into Mai's slow fuck, enjoying the long slide of pleasure and the pressure against her clit.

Mai closed her eyes and Dale mapped her features with her hands. Mai opened her mouth and sucked her fingers deep. The sensations rippling through Dale made her catch her breath.

Mai kept her pace, holding Dale on the edge, giving her enough and yet not enough to go over. She lowered her head and bit Dale's nipples, wetting the fabric with her mouth.

The roughness of the wet satin against her nipple made her cry out. "Oh. Don't tease." She groaned. "Don't tease me. You're driving me crazy. More."

Mai looked down at her, a wolfish grin spreading over her face. "Like this?" She bought their bodies together and pumped her hips into Dale. The pressure on her clit combined with the rub on her g-spot made her cry out as wetness surged from her. The slick slide of the toy against her clit when Mai changed the angle of her strokes made her gasp. Dale locked her legs at the ankles and clung to Mai. She screamed as she came again, digging her nails into Mai's back.

Dizzy with her release, Dale released Mai's hips. Mai slowed her strokes, easing Dale down, pulling out a little more each time until she freed the toy from her body. Dale raised a trembling hand and wiped the sweat-dampened hair from Mai's brow.

Mai turned her head and nuzzled Dale's palm. "Wait here." She left the bed and Dale closed her eyes. A raging sea of emotion swirled inside her. *When was the last time I was so satisfied with a lover? Have I ever been? We mesh. In so many ways. Too good. Too good to be true.* The dark voice of mistrust was back. The one that reminded her Molly had seemed perfect and Bill before that. No. Molly had not wanted to play in the bedroom. And when she was with Bill, she had been too young and inexperienced to understand the nature of her desires. When she had finally been brave enough to tell him, he told her she was sick and left her with three kids. Fear, cold and hard-edged, wormed its way into her thoughts.

"Lift your hips."

Mai's voice yanked her back to the present and Dale raised her hips.

"Down."

The roughness of terry cloth under her ass told her Mai had placed a towel under her. A warm washcloth settled between her legs.

"Let's get you cleaned up."

Dale peeped at Mai from under her lashes. "I've never done that before."

Mai tossed the washcloth in the direction of the bathroom. "It was sexy as hell." She settled her head between Dale's legs.

"I don't know if I can come again." Dale flicked Mai's hair off her forehead.

"Even if you don't it will feel good, won't it?" She kissed the inside of Dale's thigh. "Lie back."

Dale relaxed and gave over to the soothing warmth of Mai's mouth as she licked gently over her labia and her clit. A dull heat spread over her and a small flame built into slow rolling orgasm, wringing every bit of pleasure from her.

Mai hummed against her. "So sweet." She moved up and over Dale and lay next to her. She lifted her arm and settled Dale's head against her chest before she pulled the sheet over them. Dale inhaled the warm scent of Mai's skin, closed her eyes, savored the feel of Mai's strong arms encircling her, and fell asleep.

*

Mai woke to the insistent pressure of her bladder. Dale's body was curled around her, her thigh positioned over her legs. She tapped her on the shoulder.

"What?" Dale murmured against her shoulder.

"I need the facilities."

"What the hell are you talking about?" Dale raised her head.

"I need to pee."

Dale snorted and lifted herself clear of Mai. "Got it."

Mai scooted out of the bed and hurried to the bathroom. She closed the door and took care of her business. Taking a moment, she brushed her teeth.

She opened the door to the bedroom. Dale was propped up in bed. She had divested herself of her lingerie while Mai was in the bathroom. Her bare shoulders were exposed above the sheet.

Mai nipped back across the chill room and slid under the covers.

Dale slid out of the other side and headed to the bathroom. Mai lay back and studied the ceiling. *Tell her. She'll be okay. You have to do this. It's too much to leave on the table. Noah could go to school. Would she let me pay for it?*

The door to the bathroom opened. Dale had retrieved her terry cloth robe and it was tied tight around her. She tilted her head to the side and pushed back her hair. "Close your eyes."

"Again?"

"Do it."

Mai listened hard, trying to figure out Dale's movements. The bed dipped and swayed.

"Hold out your hands."

Mai held her hands out.

"Palms up, joker."

The exasperation in Dale's voice made Mai grin.

A smooth object was placed in her hands.

"Open them."

A light-brown wooden box, shaped like a heart and polished to a high shine, lay in her palms. The intricate patterns of the wood grain caught the light, making it seem as if the box glowed. "It's gorgeous." She opened the box. Inside was a folded light-blue piece of paper. Mai withdrew it and placed the box reverently on the nightstand. She glanced up and into Dale's eyes. They were dark, fear writ large in them. Mai opened the paper. "I love you" was written in large careful print.

Mai swallowed hard and looked up and into Dale's face. "You do?"

Dale sat back on her heels. "I do. I love you. And I'm sorry I didn't say it when you said it to me the first time."

Mai lifted her arm. "Come here."

Dale scooted close on the bed. Mai lifted the covers and she slid beneath them and snuggled into Mai's body.

Mai hugged her close and rested her chin on her head. "I was afraid I'd scared you off."

"Almost." Dale rested her hand on Mai's stomach.

How to tell her? Say it. It will be okay. Rip the bandage off. "I took a job in New York." Mai carded her fingers through Dale's hair. "But it's only for eight shows. I'll be gone for three months."

"You said yes?"

"You knew about the offer?

"Noah told me. But he didn't tell me you had said yes." Dale pulled the note from Mai's fingers and left the bed.

"It's only temporary. It's a special. I'll be able to pay for everything, and more."

Dale hugged her arms around herself, crumpling the note in her hand. "Guess I took too long making the box." She swept a hand through her hair and looked up at the ceiling.

Mai fought to keep her voice even. "I'll come back. It's only for three months."

"It could lead to more work, couldn't it?" Dale turned her back to Mai, her spine ramrod straight.

"Yes, it could."

"And you'll be working with Charlene. Acting like you are back together for your legion of fans to ship you?" Dale spat Charlene's name like a curse as she jammed her arms into her robe and knotted it.

Mai crossed her arms over her chest. "Yes. And what does have to do with anything? I'm a professional."

Dale turned and skewered Mai with a hard glare. "A lot." She tossed the wadded-up note into the trash can next to the door. "I get it. A big paycheck's more than I can offer you here. Don't let me hold you up." She stalked from the room.

Mai covered her face with both hands. *Should have talked with her about it. Shouldn't have waited to tell her. Fuck, what have I done? She thinks I'm like everyone else, that I'm leaving her. No.* Mai threw the covers back and left the bed. *Go after her?* She pulled her T-shirt and briefs on. *Give her time to cool off. She'll come back.*

As she dressed, she glanced back at the bed, rumpled from their lovemaking. The heart-shaped box on the side table mocked her. She rummaged in the trash can and found Dale's crumpled declaration of her love.

Mai walked back to the bed and crawled under the covers. The faint warm sleepy scent of their afternoon lovemaking surrounded her. She smoothed the note with her fingers and read it again. She lay there, hoping Dale would return, hoping she would calm down, hoping she would give Mai a chance to make her understand how much she loved her.

The gloaming turned into full dark. Dale did not return. Regret warred with anger as Mai rewound the events of the afternoon. *She's ready to give up on us. What kind of future could we have? She's done. She's too afraid to give us a chance.*

Mai sat up, refolded the paper, and placed it inside the box. After leaving the bed, she retrieved her suitcase from the closet and opened the chest of drawers that held her clothes. In fifteen minutes, her bag was packed.

Mai scanned the room to make sure she had all her belongings. The heart-shaped box was on the nightstand next to the bed. She smoothed her fingers over the lid, the wood satin-smooth under her fingertips. She picked up the box and held it to her chest a moment, wrapped it in a T-shirt, and nestled it in the middle of her suitcase. She zipped the bag closed and left the room.

Chapter Twenty-Four

"Maybe you could come here on the weekends? We could hang out. Chip's mom would let you stay with them." Noah leaned against the kitchen counter.

"Maybe. I don't know if it would be okay with your mom."

"She's super mad at you. Madder than she ever was at Molly."

Mai shrugged. "She doesn't think I'll come back. And I think she thinks I'm going to stiff her for the costs of the renovation. I can at least take care of one of those worries." Mai held out the bank envelope with the counter check in it. "Give her this. It's the rest of what I owe her plus twenty percent to cover my room and board."

"You mean couch and board." Noah frowned as she took the envelope from Mai. "You know this is going to make her mad angry?"

Mai placed both hands on the countertop. "I can't help how she feels. At least she doesn't have to worry about any bills."

Noah studied her. "If you had the money why did you take the job teaching me? And sleep on our ratty couch? The cat won't even lay on it."

Mai bit her lip. "I only have money because of three things. One, I never say no to a job, and two, I'm careful how I spend it. And three, my sister is genius at finance."

Noah placed the envelope on the counter. "You're coming back, right? To open the restaurant?"

Mai shifted her gaze from Noah's eager face. "That's the plan."

Noah's brows drew down. "But plans can change."

Mai glanced up at his sharp tone.

"I get it. I'm not a little kid." He shoved his hands in his pockets. "Thanks. For teaching me all the stuff you did. Mom said I had to wait until after graduation to look for a restaurant job. Would you write me a reference?"

"Of course, let me know where to send it."

A silence, thick with loss, rose between them. Mai crossed her arms over her aching chest. "Hey, maybe you could visit me? I'd pay for your trip. Show you the studio."

"Maybe." The blare of a car horn sounded from outside. "Gotta go." He waved awkwardly. "See ya."

Mai waited until the door closed behind him to wipe her eyes.

*

"Deal me in." Dale ruffled Noah's hair and sat down opposite Eli.

The cacophony of the brewpub irritated Dale as did most things since Mai had left. The Mai-shaped empty space in her life being the thing that irritated her the most.

Eli dealt Dale seven cards.

Thomas leaned back in his chair. "I think we should order the steak bites tonight." He waggled his eyebrows. "We are officially debt free."

Seth lifted his beer. "To being free and clear." The unsaid "thanks to Mai and her generous final payment" hung unsaid in the air between them.

Dale lifted her glass of water half-heartedly and took a sip.

"You heard from her?" Eli flipped the top card to start the game.

"No." Dale studied her hand.

"I did." Noah played a skip card and the round passed to Dale.

"What?" Dale placed her cards face down on the table. *She contacts my kid and not me? What the fuck is that all about?* "What'd she say?"

"Would you like to order your meal?" The fresh-faced waitress appeared at Dale's elbow.

"A stout, please. And no, we're not ready to order our meal yet." Dale turned back to Noah. "When?"

"She emails me." He lifted his eyebrow. "'Cause I don't have a phone."

Dale drummed her fingers on the table. She had texted with Mai only once since she had left for New York. A curt exchange, thanking her for paying in advance and telling her how unnecessary her extra payment for room and board had been.

And maybe a bit about how she wasn't a whore. And who could blame Mai for not responding to Dale's texts with anything but a short explanation and nothing else. The silence between them had been what hurt the most.

Dale had picked up her phone a dozen times to text her and put it down again every one of those times because she couldn't figure out what to say. *Why did she leave like she did if she loves me? And paid off her bill? Because I stonewalled. Like I do. And why? Why did I fall for her anyway?*

Dale had managed to keep it together, managed to keep going, but every night she lay in her empty bed and scrolled through the Hit Me Up app to see if Mai had opened her profile again. *Stalking her, like the pitiful lovesick woman I am. Fuck me.*

"Mom." Seth bumped Dale's shoulder with his own.

"What?"

"Your turn."

"Oh." Dale scanned her cards not seeing any of them.

Seth tilted his head at her. "It's okay if you don't want to play."

Dale tossed her cards aside. "Sorry guys, Dad. I'm not—I'm not feeling well. See you at home." She leveled her gaze at Seth. "Noah drives. And no arguments."

"Got it." Seth shuffled Dale's cards into the draw pile.

Eli caught her arm as she walked by his chair. "You could call her, you know?"

"I know." Dale pulled free from his grip. "I know. I don't know what to say." She pushed her hair back from her eyes.

Eli tilted his head and peered into Dale's eyes. "How about the truth? Tell her you miss her. And you love her."

"I told her I loved her. She still left. It won't change anything." A server bumped into Dale's hip and she shifted closer to her father.

"Tell her again. You need to at least give her a chance. Talk to her. Don't pretend you don't care when you do. You might not get a second chance. She's up there with a lot of young ladies who might want to soothe her broken heart and other places."

"Dad!" Dale flushed.

"It's true. And if I were you, I'd make the trip to tell her in person."

Dale turned away from her father "I'll think about it."

Across the table Seth and Noah bumped fists. She rolled her eyes as the possibility of a road trip began to shape up in her mind.

Chapter Twenty-Five

"Hey, what's up?" Mai placed her phone on speaker and moved back to the stove top to take Yvonne's call.

"Whatcha doing?"

"Heating up some leftovers."

"You have any Thanksgiving plans?"

"Tomorrow is dedicated to sweatpants, coffee, and the parade."

Yvonne's cough echoed in the apartment. "Sorry. This damn virus won't go away."

Mai turned off the flame under her soup pot. "You sound wet. Did you do your nebulizer?" A tickle of sweat ran down between Mai's shoulder blades. "Do you need me to come out there?"

"Yes, I did. And no. You need to finish out your contract."

Mai ran her hand through her hair. "Why the hell did you let me say yes to this job? I hate it. And it reminds me every day why I split with Charlene. She's so rude. How did I not see what a jerk she is?"

"You didn't even tell me about the job until you'd signed on. What the hell was I supposed to say? Oh no, Mai, don't make a fuckton of money? And about Charlene, would have you have listened?"

"I'm an idiot. I hate this. I hate being here. All I want is to be back in Sikesville."

"You mean back with Dale." Yvonne's tone was arch.

"That's over." Mai winced and picked at the countertop with her nail.

"Because she said so? Or because you bailed?"

"I bailed. And she didn't give me a chance to explain. She was super angry about the extra money I sent."

"Okay, let's review here."

Mai rolled her eyes at Yvonne's teacher voice.

"You act like you're too broke to rent a place and take her up on her offer to live in her house. Even after you start dating her you don't come clean about your finances. You tell her you love her. She says she cares. Then you take a job, without talking to anyone about it. She says she loves you and you say, that's great and all, but I'm leaving for three months to make a show with lots of pretend flirting with my ex and I have to act like we are back together so the audience can believe we are together again. And then you send her 'extra' to cover unspecified services like she's a call girl."

Mai flushed. "It sounds so bad when you put it that way."

"'Cause it is bad." Yvonne's tone gentled. "*Jiějie*, don't fuck this up. Try again. Explain about the money. Give her another chance. Give yourself one too. You love her. Don't give up easy. We have plenty of money. You need to relax about it. We will be fine. Hell, even if the restaurant never makes a dime and you didn't work another day in your life, you would have enough money. We'll have enough."

Mai's phone buzzed with a text. She moved the phone away from her ear to read the screen. Her pulse rate rocketed.

"I have to go." Mai tapped out a return text as she raced toward the bedroom and the shower.

"You okay?"

"I might be. Love you. I'll text later."

"Wait, what?"

Mai thumbed off the call and tossed her phone on the bed and stripped off her clothes as she turned on the shower.

Chapter Twenty-Six

Dale cursed the traffic and her own decision to drive her work truck to New York. After circling Mai's building for a thousand times she found a spot to wedge her truck into.

Should have texted earlier. What if she's not alone? Why did I think this would be a good idea? Fuck. Dale's hands were sweaty on the wheel. She got out, locked the truck, and walked the four blocks to Mai's building.

The doorman eyed her suspiciously while he called Mai's apartment. Dale noted the posh surroundings and shook her head at the idea Mai had spent months sleeping on her lumpy couch when she could afford to stay in a place like this. The doorman finally let her in, and she walked through the foyer of the building.

Her boots were loud on the marble floor. Fake pine wreaths wrapped with holiday ribbon reminded Dale she had not finished Christmas shopping. She swiped her wrist over the line of sweat at her hairline. Loud chimes announced the elevator's arrival. The doors opened and she stepped into the car.

The numbers flew by as it climbed the high-rise. As each floor passed, Dale was convinced she had made a huge mistake. The jolt of the elevator as it stopped on the eighteenth floor broke her out of her thoughts. The doors opened and she stepped out onto the plush carpet. At the end of the hall, Mai waited. The door to her apartment stood open behind her.

Dale swallowed her fear and forced herself to walk when all she wanted to do was run and scoop Mai into her arms and kiss her until they were both breathless.

Mai's mouth curved into a half smile. "You lost?"

Dale shook her head. "Hell of a wrong turn if I am."

Mai crossed her arms over her chest. "Social call? Or business?"

Dale stopped squarely in front of Mai. "Depends."

"On what?"

Dale latched onto the front of Mai's shirt with one hand, pulled her close, and kissed her. She dug her other hand into her wet hair and breathed in Mai's sandalwood soap and underneath it the familiar of scent of her skin. Mai circled her arms around Dale and met her kiss with the same passion. A deep groan rose from Dale. Home. Whatever else she needed to do, she needed Mai in her life.

Dale broke the kiss and held Mai's gaze. "On you. If you forgive me. I was unreasonable."

Mai brushed Dale's hair back of her shoulders. "I could have taken the time to talk to you."

"We hadn't agreed to that kind of thing."

Mai kissed the corner of Dale's mouth. "We didn't talk about a lot of things."

Dale rested her hands on Mai's chest. "I love you, Mai Li. I want you in my life. Whatever it takes, I'll do it."

Mai rested her hand on Dale's and cupped the back of her neck. She leaned her forehead against her brow. "I've missed you. Every damn day I was here. All I could think about was how soon I could get back to you. And how to get you back."

"You never lost me." Dale looped her arms around Mai's neck.

"Come inside? Or were you planning on throwing me in the truck and driving me back home tonight?"

Dale leaned back into Mai's embrace. "I have all weekend." She frowned. "But I'm probably going to have to move my truck."

Mai took Dale's hand and pulled her inside the open apartment. "Later." She tugged Dale into a hard kiss and kicked the door closed.

They stumbled toward the living room. Mai kissed her way along Dale's neck. "I missed you. So much." She unzipped Dale's jacket and slipped her hands inside. Dale moved her hands into Mai's hair and tugged her closer. She licked the sweet shell of her ear. "I couldn't stay angry. I tried."

"I'm sorry. I should have told you. About the money and everything. I didn't want things to change between us."

Dale shivered as Mai shoved her jacket down over her shoulders and tossed it aside. "I get it. I know what it's like to trust the wrong person and lose everything."

Mai rested her head on Dale's shoulder. "It's not that I didn't trust you, I didn't want to leave. I didn't think you wanted what I wanted. Living with you was a way to pretend you did."

Dale moved back to raise Mai's head. "What do you want, Mai?"

"You. Long-term. Not a hookup."

Dale frowned and a flush of knowing spread across her face. "You thought I only wanted your body. Because of the app."

Mai bit her lip. "I'm in love with you, Dale. I can't pretend I'm not." Mai hung her head. "Even if it's not what you want, I want what I can have with you, as messed up as that sounds."

Dale cupped Mai's face and kissed her brow, her cheeks, and finally her mouth gently. "I wouldn't have driven in the worst fucking traffic on the Wednesday before Thanksgiving for a hookup. I want you in my life. All of you. Not just the sexy bits. I love how you are with my kids and my crazy father. I love how you treat me as if I'm the most precious woman in the universe. I want you. All of you. Every day. I know you have to stay for now, but will you come back to me when you're finished?"

Mai gazed into Dale's eyes. "I've never left you." She lifted Dale's hand to her mouth and kissed her fingertips.

"Do you have to be anywhere today?" Dale eyed the clock display on the stovetop.

A half smile curved up Mai's mouth. "Nope. But I think we need to move your truck to the building's parking garage. This place comes with two spaces."

"We need to move it now?"

"Yes." Mai picked up Dale's jacket and handed it to her. "Once I get you the way I want you, I'm not going to want to move for a long time."

Dale raised her eyebrow. "And how is it you want me?" She rubbed her thumb over Mai's lower lip.

"Naked and in my bed."

Dale jingled her keys and held them out to Mai. "Let's go."

Chapter Twenty-Seven

SPRING

"Hey, watch it!" Noah snatched the football out of the air a split second before it connected with Mai's ass. "Mom!"

His disconcerted expression made Dale laugh. "Sorry. My bad."

Mai turned around and skewered Dale with her gaze. "Thank you, Noah, for saving my dignity."

Dale jogged over to Mai and wrapped her arms around her. She brought her lips close to Mai's ear and whispered, "If I had pegged you with the football, I would have had an excuse to rub it and make it better."

Mai looped her fingers in the belt loops of Dale's jeans and tugged her close. "Like you need an excuse to rub my ass?" She nuzzled Dale's neck.

"Get a room." Yvonne's teasing tone broke the moment. Whistles and hoots from Ida and Jeff and her father coupled with laughter from Noah and his brothers added to the cacophony. Sally clapped and Chip blushed.

Dale tilted her head sideways. "All right, you comedians. Let's get this party started." She lifted the bottle of non-alcoholic cider and waggled it.

Yvonne held out her cup and Dale filled it. She raised her glass toward the group. "To old friends and new ones, well met." She arched a brow at Sally. Sally touched her cup to Yvonne's and sat down next to her on the blanket, inclining her body toward Yvonne. Yvonne rested her fingertips on Sally's arm as they chatted. Dale nudged Mai and tilted her head toward the two women, their infatuation with each other obvious to Dale. Mai shrugged and took another sip of her cider.

Dale rested her arm around Mai's waist. The sun shone off the lake and ducks squawked and flapped on the far side of the shore. A breeze rippled across the water. The low hum of their families as they ate the picnic Mai had prepared was background noise to the hammering of Dale's heart. This was precious. Family and friends. How much could change in a year. She patted her watch pocket to reassure herself the ring was still there.

"You okay?" Mai raised her eyebrows. "Walk with me?" Mai stood up and walked backward as she held out her hand.

Dale caught up to her and took her hand and laced their fingers together. They walked over the beach toward the dock on the other end of the lake. A flutter of nerves settled in her stomach. The dock, site of their first time together, and a few more since the weather had broken, loomed in the distance. It wasn't what Dale had planned but it would do.

Mai led them to the end of the dock. She sat down and patted the worn gray wood next to her.

Dale sat next to her, thigh to thigh. A dozen memories of their time together rushed through her thoughts. She gripped Mai's thigh to keep her hand from trembling. *What if she says no? What if it's too soon. Fuck.*

"You feeling frisky? Because I don't think we are far enough from our families to risk it." Mai's teasing grin as she placed her hand high on Dale's thigh and squeezed her leg reminded Dale of every reason why she loved her.

"They've been like barnacles all day." Mai released Dale's thigh and leaned back on her elbows. "I thought I'd never get you alone." She held Dale's hand in both of hers. "Do you want to get married?"

"What?" Dale flushed and gripped Mai's hand.

"Do you want to get married? To me?" Mai tilted her head.

"Yes."

"Are you sure?" Mai held her gaze.

"Of course, why would I say yes if I wasn't sure?" Dale frowned at Mai.

Mai dug a velvet-covered box from her pocket and opened it. The solid black silicone band was dark against the white satin. "It's a safety ring, no worries about shocks or anything."

Dale stared at the band and then lifted her gaze to Mai's face. "Are you sure?"

Mai raised her eyebrow. "For fuck's sake, why would I ask if I wasn't sure?"

Dale huffed out a breath. "I didn't expect this."

Mai frowned. "What's wrong?"

"I wanted to ask you."

"You want a do-over, my sweet control freak?"

Dale rolled her eyes. "No." She took the ring from the box and held it out to Mai. "Put it on me?"

Mai pushed the ring over her knuckle and then kissed her fingers. Dale cupped Mai's face and kissed her slowly. Mai broke their kiss, her eyes shining. "Were you really going to ask me?"

Dale tapped the lump in her jeans pocket. "I had plans to get down on one knee."

Mai pushed the hair back from her eyes. "That sounds delightful. Maybe later we can have a do-over. I like it when you get down on your knees."

"Perv."

Mai picked up her hand and pressed a kiss to the palm. "Yeah, but I'm your perv now."

She looked over Dale's shoulder at their gathered families on the beach. "So, are we going to tell them, or keep it between us?"

Dale traced her finger over Mai's lips. "No secrets."

"Never?"

Dale raised her eyebrow. "Exceptions made for surprise parties and gifts?"

"Deal."

Mai brushed her lips over Dale's mouth. "Deal."

A shout from the crowd on the beach drew their attention. They followed the line of their vision. A large purple kite with rainbow streamers rose on the wind, climbing higher in the clear blue sky.

Dale touched Mai's chin. "Did you know last year when we flew kites, I wanted you?"

Mai smirked. "I might have had a clue. I could see you in the truck sideview mirror."

Dale face burned. "Fuck."

Mai kissed her, lingering on her lower lip. "It was sexy as hell. And I wanted you to throw me in the back of the truck and have your way with me."

Dale leaned her brow against her forehead. "I can't believe you want to marry me."

Mai hugged her tight. "Were you worried I'd say no?"

She rested her hand in the curve of Mai's shoulder. "Yes. It's a lot to take on. Three boys, even if only two of them live with us. We're a pretty tight family."

Mai pushed back to look in Dale's eyes. "You see how I am with Yvonne? Family is what's important. A marriage is adding to a family, not taking away."

Dale hooked her fingers in Mai's belt loops, pulled her close, and kissed her. More whooping from the beach made her look over Mai's shoulder. "Did you tell them you planned this?"

"I might have mentioned it."

Dale quirked her mouth. "You're know you're stuck with me now? No take backs."

"No take backs." Mai slid her hand in the back pocket of Dale's jeans and tugged her close. "Let's give them something more to cheer about."

Acknowledgements

This book is the first in a new series that came about after a discussion on The Lesbian Review Chat Group on Facebook. Readers listed things they would like to see in lesbian romance. I took notes, so VT, this one is for you. Cate was my inspiration for Dale. There will be more, but I couldn't fit everything in the first book.

About the Author

Brenda Murphy (she/her) writes erotic romance. Her most recent novel, *Double Six,* is a 2020 Golden Crown Literary Society award finalist, and *Knotted Legacy*, the third book in the Rowan House series, made the 2018 The Lesbian Review's Top 100 Vacation Reads list. You can catch her musings on writing, books, and living with wicked ADHD on her blog Writing While Distracted. She loves sideshows and tattoos and yes, those are her monkeys. When she is not loitering at her local library, she wrangles twins, one dog, and an unrepentant parrot

I hope you enjoy reading this book as much as I enjoyed writing it. For a free short story, information on book signings, appearances, work in progress snippets, previews and sneak-peeks, sign up for my email list at:

Website: www.brendalmurphy.com

Facebook: www.facebook.com/Writing-While-Distracted

Twitter: @bmurphysideshow

Other NineStar books by this author

Dominique and Other Stories

One

The Rowan House series
Sum of the Whole
Both Ends of the Whip
Knotted Legacy
Complex Dimensions
Double Six

With Megan Hart
Soul Burn

Coming Soon from Brenda Murphy

Lockset

University Square, Book Two

Eunice Park glared at the ringing phone on her desk. On the third ring she picked it up. "What is it?"

"Sorry to bother you, Eunice, but your father's on the line. He insisted I connect him."

Eunice leaned forward and straightened her posture. "What?"

"Your father. Says it's urgent. Want me to take a message? Or leave him on hold till he hangs up?"

Eunice swept her hair back with one hand and closed her fist around it, barely resisting the urge to tear it out. "No. I'll talk to him." She took her reading glasses off and tossed them on the top of the stack of trial transcripts and depositions on her desk.

"Eun?" James Park's rich baritone filled her ear. Her Korean name, spoken in the way it was meant to be said, made her heart squeeze. She detested Eunice and still cursed the day she had chosen to use it instead of her true name.

"Yes." She pinched the bridge of her nose. "It's me."

Silence stretched out between them, harsh and violent. Eun settled back into her chair. Her father's silence and its power over Eun had weakened over the years. Eun knew his trick. Wait for the other to become so uncomfortable they spilled their secrets and told you everything you wanted to know. For once, Eun would not give in. She set her gaze on the clock on her computer screen. One minute. Two minutes. Eun fiddled with the edge of her blotter.

At three-and one-half minutes her father cleared his throat and spoke. "Come home. I need to see you."

"Nothing's changed." Eun chewed her lip.

"I need to see you."

"Why now? I'm not coming home to be berated again. You made yourself clear five years ago. I'm not backing down. Not this time."

"I'm not asking you to. I have something to discuss with you. I can't do it over the phone. Please. This weekend?"

Eun rubbed her forehead. "I can't. I'm buried. I have dog of a case, my cocounsel is an idiot, and I've got closing arguments next week. The weekend after?"

"If that's the best you can do."

"What?" Eun's voice rose as anger she had managed to contain bubbled up. "Oh hell no. You can't call me up out of the blue, demand I see you, and then act all pissy if I can't drop what I'm doing and run home. Not after what you pulled last time. I'm lesbian, Dad. I've been lesbian, I'm going to be lesbian. Nothing is going to change that."

"I know." The defeated tone in his voice scraped against Eun's battered heart.

"I have to go."

"Will you come?"

"Next weekend."

Her father disconnected the call. Eun fell back into her chair. Late afternoon sun raked the tops of the high-rise buildings surrounding the office building. Red-and-orange light, reflected off the glass, shone through the floor to ceiling window and glinted off the framed print on the wall opposite her desk.

Her stomach rumbled, an audible reminder of her neglecting to eat breakfast and lunch. She tapped her pen on the desk and glowered at the stack of transcripts on her desk as she rang her assistant. "Order us some food, please.'

"Have a hankering for anything?" Sally's soft drawl spilled through the phone.

"Whatever you want."

"You okay?"

"I will be."

Also Available from NineStar Press

Connect with NineStar Press

www.ninestarpress.com

www.facebook.com/ninestarpress

www.facebook.com/groups/NineStarNiche

www.twitter.com/ninestarpress